# BLIND BEAST MATE

BEAST MATES, #1

MILANA JACKS

This is a work of fiction. Names, characters, businesses, places, events and incidents are either the products of the author's imagination or used in a fictitious manner. Unless you've seen alien beasts in the grocery store, any resemblance to actual persons, living or dead, or actual events is purely coincidental.

# CHAPTER 1

## *Rey*

A gentle hand landed on my bare shoulder. By the size of her hand, the way she touched me, and her strong gardenia-laced perfume, I knew it was my stepmother, Leslie. "How are you holding up?" she said.

Faked affection. I held my tongue and placed the small wooden box she handed me inside my black leather backpack. "I've been better." I was holding up, or down, depending on how I regarded the forces of nature, just fine. Gravity did the work for me. Holding upward, or up, wasn't the problem, but holding on to the contents of my stomach when the bike engines—the sounds of my grim future—rumbled above the roof was a problem. The beasts circled above our community. I swallowed bile, didn't want to vomit on my alien soon-to-be husband. "Leslie, do you know if Uncle told him—"

"Shh, your uncle is here." She whispered for my benefit,

as if I couldn't hear Sam's heavy footsteps. He'd walked with a limp ever since my dad shot him in the leg, before my uncle killed him. Go, Daddy, I thought. Two months after Uncle Sam killed my dad and took over the Beast Pairing Program, he'd arranged an alien beast husband for me, his greatest burden. *"At least you weren't sold to the lowest of their ranks,"* he'd comforted me. At least he hadn't killed me, I comforted myself. He'd killed Dad for not punishing my sister for running away from her beast pair my dad had sold her to. The same day he'd killed my sister.

After massacring my family, Uncle Sam did me a favor and allowed me to say good-bye to them. He'd put the bodies in glamorous coffins for the viewing I couldn't view. Asshole. For the past two months, I'd nursed fears of abandonment, fears of what Uncle Sam would do with me, while smiling for the sake of his new wife—who was my dad's ex-wife and the mother of my dead sister. Leslie had broken out of one abusive marriage with my dad to enter another with his brother, my Uncle Sam. She pillow-talked my uncle into killing my father for not punishing my sister. She hadn't anticipated Uncle Sam would shoot my sister too. I hated Leslie.

A tear slid down my cheek, and I wiped it with a shaking hand. I didn't want to be paired with an alien beast man, because he'd expect a perfect wife, something the communities had provided for the alien race ever since they'd occupied Earth. I didn't have any choice in the matter. If the Alpha Beast hadn't bought me, someone else would have. The Alpha Beast was the most inhuman of them all. They said he ate his bedmates. *Why me?*

"Did Sam tell my husband about me?" I whispered to Leslie, mindful of Sam's approaching steps.

"I doubt it. We celebrated with the beasts all night. I'm exhausted. Pretend to be normal for as long as you can. If the Alpha comes to like you, he'll keep you, but if he returns you and requests a refund, I won't be able to save you, the same way I couldn't save your sister. Sam won't listen to me. I'm sorry." Her soft touch left my shoulder, and her heels clicked across the tiled floors.

"Rey," Uncle Sam said and placed a heavy hand on my shoulder. "He's here. Rode in with the entire city."

Uncle Sam was jealous. The beasts didn't outnumber us humans, but after the Great Nuclear War, which destroyed most of the Earth, the human survivors had closed themselves off and formed private communities. Stuck inside the confines of our communities, the human race fragmented, and we forgot about each other. The beasts had occupied the Earth in all of one night before the community's leaders surrendered, and after the aliens discovered some of us could breed with them, the Beast Pairing Program was born.

Uncle Sam gripped my elbow and tugged. I faced the short, stocky man and forced a smile that amounted to a show of teeth. Beside my leg, Dark, my guide hound, growled low in his throat. Despite his dislike for Uncle Sam, he didn't bite. His spiky fur brushed my leg as he rose to standing and guided me down the hallway leading outside. Before the exit, I tugged my elbow away from Sam's grip.

Uncle Sam pushed me against the wall. *Here he goes again.* But I couldn't have cared less. The only thing on my mind was the Alpha Beast. I hoped I didn't look too nervous to meet him. I hoped I didn't vomit when I did meet him. And now, I hoped the giggle that escaped my lips didn't match my hound's snarl. Uncle Sam squeezed my elbow and pressed his body against mine. He was only an inch or two taller than my five foot nine, and the stale beer breath hit my nose when he said, "Make him happy. If he returns you because he expected a trophy wife and not a blind bitch, I'll put a bullet in your useless head. This community depends on their money and on pretty girls like you, so spread your legs the minute you hear his belt unsnap. Your momma must've taught you something."

The Alpha Beast, my husband, didn't know I'd been removed from the Pairing Program after my accident. I hadn't expected Uncle Sam to tell him, but again, I'd hoped he'd honor my dad's wishes to keep me at home and not sell me no matter how pretty I was. Also, I'd hoped the Alpha would ask someone about me before buying me. He hadn't. I hoped far too much. Fat chance he'd want to marry me if he'd asked. The beasts called us their pairs, and they expected perfect, genetically compatible women who'd give them strong offspring. Trouble with me? I could barely take care of myself, let alone any offspring.

I scrunched up my nose and suppressed a gag at Uncle Sam's breath and my situation. "You shouldn't have arranged a pairing with anyone, let alone with a beast you all fear would destroy you," I said. "I offered to work the kitchens and earn my keep."

"The beast came and saw you watering the damn plants. He asked about you, so I paired you off. Good riddance, and by the way he kept watching you, I'd say he figured a pretty young thing like you would make any man happy."

"You must really hate him," I said, joking at my own expense. I was pretty good at finding the bright side.

"Everyone hates the Alpha Beast."

Motorcycles rumbled in the yard as the beasts descended from the sky.

Uncle Sam stepped back when the engine noise died and hard-hitting boots over gravel approached.

"Thank you, Sam," I said and gripped Dark's leash. "It was nice knowing you. I hope you die a slow and painful death." Usually, I wasn't so bold with Sam since he'd swung at me and I lost most of my eyesight due to head trauma, but I figured he deserved far worst parting words than those. I hadn't told anyone it was him who'd hit me. I said I fell out of the window and cracked my head on a rock. An accident. He'd kill me if I told the truth.

Sam placed his hand on my throat and took Dark's leash. Immediately, my hound barked in protest. A thwack sounded, and Dark yelped.

I wanted this man to meet his Maker. "Give me the leash."

"Can't do. No place for hounds on bikes, just bitches. Put your fucking sunglasses on. Your eyes are on my forehead."

A large, dark silhouette entered our sanctuary. I couldn't see a whole lot, but I saw silhouettes and blurry contrast. I stopped tugging the leash.

I presumed it was the Alpha Beast but wasn't sure, so I said nothing and slid my sunglasses over my eyes. I clenched my shaking hands.

"You're right on time. I was just telling your wife—"

"My pair," the Alpha Beast corrected in a deep baritone voice, which suited his massive frame. It sent a shiver down my spine. I'd seen a man-beast before I lost my sight. A cross between a man and a wolf. A humanoid monster with an enormous chest, and claws and teeth made for ripping into flesh.

Uncle Sam cleared his throat. "I told your pair how lucky she was. Here you go, honey," Uncle Sam said and threaded my hands through the straps of my backpack. "Packed small like a good girl. Wants to take her hound."

The Alpha Beast grunted. "No hounds." He took my hand in his large callused one and pulled. I followed behind him, grateful for his guidance. Little did he know, I hardly saw where I stepped. The voices of his beasts and the smell of cigarette smoke grew closer as the Alpha Beast dragged me across the community's yard. Abruptly, we stopped, and I ran into the back of his arm. It was like hitting a wall. "Oomph," I muttered and bounced off, one leg stretched far back to prevent a fall. I guessed we'd reached his bike when the Alpha Beast released my hand. I didn't move.

Dark barked with abandon, and I turned toward his voice. I had to have my hound with me. For one, I didn't know what Uncle Sam would do with him, and two, I depended on Dark to get me around, especially now when I didn't know where the hell I was going. I opened my mouth to ask my husband—*pair, I should call him pair*—to reconsider when he slid my backpack off my shoulders. A clawed fingertip lifted my chin. I managed to turn up my lips. A cold leather collar snapped around my neck. My collar. It was a beast thing. I was an owned pair.

"Thank you," I said, "It's beautiful."

The Alpha Beast grunted. A large hand framed one side of my face, and his mouth slammed down on mine, his tongue demanding entrance. Whistling and hooting followed his assault—he considered it a kiss, I was sure. His hand wound around my hair, and I could do nothing but let him invade. I pretended it was a romantic wedding kiss, a press of lips, subtle and gentle for the sake of an audience, but the Alpha clearly didn't know what gentle meant. My back nearly snapped when he leaned forward and I leaned back. He deepened the kiss. For a second, I thought, he might swallow me whole. When his tongue swirled with mine and a low growl rumbled in the back of his throat, I stopped thinking altogether.

The Alpha Beast tasted fresh, a hint of mint and lemon on his expert tongue, not a trace of stale beer or someone else's night-before lipstick. Growing up with a community whore had taught me to appreciate the small things and rejoice in those small things even at the most terrifying moments. I didn't know what would happen to me with this man, but at least he didn't taste bad on my sensitive palate.

After a minute, his kissing slowed and his tongue stopped moving. Not knowing what else to do, I stroked it with mine. With the tip of my tongue, I flicked his. The Alpha Beast groaned into my mouth and pressed me closer. He was so hard, I thought he might burst out of his pants and take me right over his bike. He could do what he wanted with me. I was his pair.

His lips left mine. My mouth still gaped, and my lips tingled from rubbing on his stubble. I'd never been taken like this before. The Alpha Beast chuckled, probably at my gaping mouth, and his rough, two-day-unshaven cheek brushed my soft one as his sharp teeth nibbled my ear. He whispered, "Your uncle swore to me you are a virgin. Swore up and down nobody's spoiled you, and charged me an arm and a leg for your virginal pussy. Let's be clear in case you aren't. Tell me now so I don't gotta drive back to collect his arm and a leg."

I wasn't a virgin, but I'd protected myself from abuse. In fact, I was so good at protecting myself that I traded rape trauma for a life of blindness. A trade no woman should have to make. I swiped away those memories and focused on the now.

The silence in the yard never sounded louder. I estimated that between his beasts and the community's humans, about three hundred people watched and listened. Even Dark had stopped barking. "Can we talk about this later?" I whispered.

"No. Answer me."

My body was still bent back, and he appeared a dark mass against the lit sky. I gripped the back of his head and tried to pull him down so I could whisper in his ear. I tugged, but he didn't budge. Okay, then. "Maybe," I said.

"Twenty says there be bloody sheets!" someone shouted.

I would've liked to keep our business private.

The Alpha Beast straightened, and three hard thumps sounded. He might've thumped his chest, but I wasn't sure. It sounded suspiciously like something a gorilla did. He picked me up and plopped my ass on the back of his bike. The way he manhandled me suited me fine. He could move me from one place to the next all he wanted. Next, he removed my sunglasses and paused.

Minutes passed, and I barely hitched breaths.

"You're beautiful," he said and placed my sunglasses in my backpack so the helmet fit over my head.

Dark barked.

Soft paws padded over gravel.

They landed on my thigh at the same time the Alpha Beast straddled his bike. I found Dark's head and scratched behind his fluffy ears. He kept barking. If my heart could split in half, it would've.

"No hounds," the Alpha Beast said. "I got a cat at home."

"Please, it would mean the world to me if you found a place for him."

"No hound." He revved the engines and prepared to lift off.

I panicked and hopped off his bike. I stood there in my darkness in the middle of the day, my heart threatening to burst out of my chest. I'd committed a sin. When a beast placed a bitch on the bike in front of his beasts, she'd better not leap off in defiance. I clenched my fists and remembered Uncle Sam's threat. I couldn't tell the Alpha Beast why I needed my hound, or he might leave me here. Or get rid of me himself.

The Alpha Beast didn't say anything right away, probably because he was too busy thinking about yanking my hair and forming words that would say *don't ever do that again*. He'd paid a fortune for me. "What the fuck are you doin'? Get back on the bike."

And there it was. "I can't leave my hound."

"I told you, I got a cat. Can't have—"

I cut him off. "Dark is well behaved. He won't—"

"Where the hell should I put the damn hound?"

"In one of your space cars. Besides, I have more stuff than what's in my backpack."

"Smartass!" the beast who'd bet a twenty shouted.

"You'll buy new stuff in Beast City," he said.

"Thank you, but—"

The Alpha Beast snarled, and I pressed my lips closed. "You got a car?" he bit out.

"No."

"Then get back on the bike right this second."

I knelt and hugged Dark. If I stayed here, my life was over. If I told the Alpha Beast he'd paired and paid a fortune for a girl who wasn't a virgin and couldn't see, my life was over. If my life was over, they'd bury Dark with me. But if we parted ways, I'd live, and when the gates to our community slid open, Dark would run out and join the many stray hound packs. He was such a good boy. "I'm sorry, boy. Run, it's better than staying here." Before I left my home, I unsnapped his leash.

# CHAPTER 2

## *Rey*

The beasts operated out of Beast City, about two hours away from our community. Beast City was built on top of the place once known as the City of Angels. The drive went smoothly. When we slowed down and my stomach almost caught in my throat from the steep descent, I knew we'd left the main space way and the bikes were preparing to land inside the city. The beasts traveled by air and not by ground like us.

Even at sundown, the heat beat down with fury and the winds picked up speed. I cried as quietly as a mouse, lest he felt my sobs on his broad back. I gripped his jacket and bit my lip when I thought about Dark. I hoped he remembered the stray ways he'd had before I'd found him and took him inside the community. I hoped he remembered how to hunt for food.

*Why me?* I asked myself for the millionth time. I wasn't even sure how the Alpha Beast accepted a pair from my family's stock, seeing as he could've gone into any community in search of a pretty pair without having to deal with Uncle Sam. Pretty girls could be found anywhere.

The Alpha Beast placed his hand over both of mine and held firm. "Hey, you wanna spin?"

"What?" I shouted over the wind in my ears as we descended.

"Don't worry, gravity's got your back. Hang on!"

Headfirst, we dived. He spun the bike in the air. We rolled, descending, and I screamed at the top of my lungs.

The Alpha Beast stopped briefly. My stomach rose, and when I thought I'd vomit for certain this time, my stomach settled with a thump. The bike's exhaust whooshed. We landed with a real soft thud, as if nothing had happened.

I clutched his middle. "Is it over?"

He shut off the engines and laughed. "Get used to it. Got you a small bike at home. Gonna take you spinnin'."

"Oh, that's wonderful," I said.

"Welcome. Let's move."

Quickly, behind his back, I checked the time. I opened my braille watch's cover and ran my fingertips over the small dots and the minute and hour hands. It was eight forty. I closed the cover and dismounted with a wince. I hadn't ridden a space bike before, and I rubbed the numbness out of my ass.

"Need help?" he asked.

I shook my head.

Funny beast.

The smell of roast beef and fumes reached my nose at the same time the beasts around us shut off their engines and called for a party. A party? My insides rolled again. They'd spill tonight, I was sure of it.

The Alpha Beast dismounted and took my hand in his.

Faced with completely unfamiliar surroundings, I gripped it for dear life.

"Home sweet home," he said and walked with long strides. I jogged with a big grin on my face in case his people watched us. A happy bride. "We'll stay only a few hours," he continued. "Eat some, drink some, get to know your new family. The works." He wanted to celebrate his pairing when I wanted him to leave me at my new home. Alone. The bright side? Maybe he'd get drunk and pass out. Or maybe he'd get drunk, forget about me, and use a beast girl instead.

The beasts had ravenous sexual appetites, and their women would know how to please their males best. Either one of the two options would work for me, if only for tonight. I wasn't in good-wife mode just yet. I wanted to explore my new house. Alone. So that I could find my way around the house, mainly a way to escape. I didn't know if I could manage an escape, but I sure couldn't sit on my ass, awaiting my fate.

We crossed a short expanse of concrete, went through a large building, and then my sensible heels dug into the soft grass all the way to the source of the loud music, barbecued ribs, alcohol, and laughter. Grass was a commodity on Earth. The beasts did what they could to revive our planet. We'd ravaged our resources before the beasts came, and they gave nature a second chance. I was born into this world, but I'd read our history and seen the pictures of California grass before the Great Nuclear War.

I squeezed his hand tighter, balanced and counted my steps as we crossed the yard. If I had to use a bathroom, I'd need to find my way back inside, wander the hallways until I found small doors somewhere in the back. In the community's main hall, the bathrooms lined the walls before the back exits.

I was on step ten, the Alpha Beast's sixth when he said, "Don't worry." *Twelve, thirteen, fourteen.* "I won't let you out of my sight. Even with my collar on, I don't trust any of these motherfuckers. I have the most beautiful pair on Earth, and here I have over seventy single, dirty, horny bastards." He chuckled.

Despite his words, I was pretty sure he trusted every last one of them, and I loved the collar, even if I found it suitable for hounds. The leather on the collar smelled new. I touched a small heart pendant that dangled from the middle. *Sixteen, seventeen, and a left turn.* Most girls in the pairing program had issues with collars, but I knew the importance of ownership with the beasts. If you weren't owned in the city, you were anyone's and anyone's girls got passed around. At least he wouldn't pass me around.

On step twenty, we stopped. The Alpha Beast sat down with me on his lap. He arranged my legs, then placed them on the bench, and his left hand slapped the table, his upper arm bracing my back.

A hand snuck into my hair and released my hair clip. Just as well, it was hanging by a thread since the ride anyhow.

My long, brown curls draped over his arm.

He did something, maybe brought it to his nose, because he said, "Smells like heaven."

I smiled.

"Don't gimme that fake smile. I've seen you give a plant a more sincere smile. You don't wanna be here, do you?"

No sense in lying. I was so nervous. My palms sweated, and with his superior senses, he might even be able to smell my fear. "Where is here?" I asked.

"The beast compound. Our sanctuary, if you will."

"I see. It's not that I don't want to be here," I clarified, "just not tonight. Maybe in a few nights, when I've found my way around...the city."

"I don't want to be here no more than you do, but I got to show face." He rearranged me on his lap. I felt him grow. He didn't hide it. He moved me over his erection. "Baby, I'm gonna try to be nice tonight. You looking forward to it? I bet you are. I bet that's why you wanna go home, to get to know your beast. I bet you're wondering how big I am, if it's gonna fit into your tight pussy. Are you wondering?"

"Yes," I muttered on a mission not to lie. How big was a monster cock?

"Let me tell ya, I'll make it fit."

Oh. How comforting. As comforting as my mother's promises of one last drink. I shuddered.

He bit my earlobe. "I will not fuck you. I will mount you like a beast male mounts a beast bitch in heat, you hear me? I've never wanted a woman more in my entire life, so get used to it. The sooner you do, the better it'll be for you."

I cleared my throat. "Maybe in a few days after I make you dinner first. I'm an excellent cook, and we'd get to know each other before—"

"Got ribs, burgers, chicken right here. You hungry?"

"I didn't mean right now, but—"

"Got a cake coming. You'll have some. What do you say?"

"Yes, Alpha Beast."

"Jamie, my name is Jamie."

*Jamie*. Such a sweet name. It didn't fit.

As the crowds came to congratulate us on our pairing, Jamie grunted along. And while he happily grunted and hit his chest at least twice, I tried to match everyone's names with their voices. It was difficult. Most beast men's voices were identically hoarse, sort of like they'd chain-smoked all their lives. Only four beast women approached, so they were easier to tell apart. I worked though my new family, the feel of their hands and the brush of women's soft skin on mine when they kissed my cheeks. I identified at least three Southern beasts by their accents.

Minutes passed, and nobody else came. I guessed we were done with congratulations. Sighted people didn't tap tables with their hands; they looked to see if there was something there. I didn't want to spill anything. I removed my backpack and placed it on the table. When glasses didn't crash, I dug inside for my sunglasses. For one, the strobe lights on the roof of the compound shone brightly over the backyard, and two, people expected eye contact. Even if I was shy—and I wasn't—I'd have to make *some* eye contact. I'd been avoiding his for most of the night.

Sunglasses worn at night weren't an unusual sight, so I slid them on.

"Hi, I'm Karen," a woman said. "I run the bar around here."

"Rey," I said and followed her voice with a smile. I tied my backpack, busied my hands in case she extended one of hers.

"Can I get you a drink?"

"Yes, please, I'll have whatever Jamie's having."

"Jamie, is it?" she said.

Hm. "It is."

A man sat next to us. His pants—presumably black jeans—brushed the tips of my sandals. "Be on your way," the twenty-dollar-bet man said, "and come back with something hard for me."

Now I knew Karen either wasn't anyone's pair or she

was this man's pair. I put my dollar on the former. I'd been around enough to know. My mother hustled in a man's world, after all.

"Vice," the man said.

He might be introducing himself to me. *Oh God, help me.* "Vice for vice president?" I asked and stretched out my hand. This was better than him extending his, because I knew where my hand was.

"Vice for wicked." Soft lips touched the top of my hand, and I exhaled in relief. He *was* introducing himself. Under my sunglasses, I blinked at his elegant gesture and didn't withdraw from his soft grip. I wondered if he wore tailored pants. The beasts came in all shapes and sizes. This one might wear nice clothes. A gentleman. Under my fingertips, Vice's skin was smooth, and I thought I might be right on track with the suit thing.

Jamie worked with his hands. They were callused, and it suited his jeans attire. I disliked generalizing, but I had nothing else to help paint a picture of my husband. I wondered what he did every day, or if he even held a day job. A job would take him away from home. It would give me some breathing room. At least for now.

## CHAPTER 3

*Jamie*

I'd almost kidnapped Rey straight out of her home, put her on my bike, and driven her to my house. That was how crazy I'd been when I first saw her smile. For us—the beasts from faraway planet Tineya— mating was a simple process. You saw a female, you felt she was your female, you took the female and made her yours. Making her yours meant conquering her pussy with might, fucking her to oblivion to get her into heat. That was our whole purpose as mated male beasts. To conquer our mate's pussy and get our mates pregnant with little beast babies.

We never told the communities we depended on their females for mating. We couldn't tell them we needed *the* girl and not any girl. We'd told them we took girls as pairs as if we could choose between many, even went as far as buying random women and putting them in the cities. It kept the power in our hands, or they'd try to fuck with us. Or hurt our mates.

Vice—the ass—had lost his mate before he'd even claimed her. We'd been looking for her all over this godforsaken land. We came to Rey's community in search of Vice's mate but found mine instead. I couldn't get Rey out of my mind, and the fact her uncle wouldn't let her talk to us, wouldn't let her join us for lunch, made me want to kidnap her even more.

I didn't ask him to pair her with me the same day. Instead, I'd listened to my brother Vice when he'd advised against mixing with scum the likes of her uncle. He'd said to be certain Rey was mine before asking for her. I went back home and couldn't get a wink of shut-eye all night. What if she ran off like Vice's mate had, and I couldn't find her? Naturally, this idea made me crazy.

Early the next day, I yanked one of their priests out of his bed so he could draw up the pairing papers. I rode back to her community with said papers and a case of money I'd strapped to my bike. Her uncle, the greedy bastard, had taken all of five minutes to sign the papers and take the money, but he held my mate for another week. Motherfucker.

But she was here now.

I buried my nose in her hair and inhaled a peach shampoo scent. I bet her pussy tasted like peaches too. My mouth watered. When I lifted my head, Vice brushed his thumb over the smooth skin of the top of her hand. My eyes turned silver-white, and my canines elongated. Slowly. My brother loved fucking with me. Or he wanted to die.

I tugged her hand away. "Vice, my brother, fuck off about a foot away." Vice laughed, and my mate chuckled. "Something funny?" I asked.

She shook her head.

I pinched her thigh.

"Ouch."

Ten minutes later, Karen, one of the natives I'd asked Vice not to keep around, brought me tchai, a cold green sweet drink with peppermint. The tchai plant from Tineya grew pretty well on Earth. I didn't drink alcohol, not after my youngest brother flipped, drunk on his bike. Went down from a few thousand feet and splattered on the green grass we'd just finished planting that year. Just like that. Gone. Me? Fuck no. I had a mate to take care of and fuck real good so we could have babies. No alcohol and riding for me.

Rey tasted her drink. Again, she tried to fake a smile. But I'd seen her smiles when they were genuine so I knew she wasn't all that into it. She probably hoped I'd have a bottle of whiskey or at least a case of beer and that I'd pass out. Lots of beasts drank, especially during their pairing party. We called it a mating party, but with natives at our compound and in the city in general, we'd adapted our customs. Earth's natives couldn't know we needed the mates they provided to reproduce. They feared us. As they should.

Rey still sipped her tchai but finally scrunched up her nose. Nope, definitely didn't like my sweet drink. The plant was a native of my planet, not hers, and I liked it real sweet. I liked many sweet things, so I licked her neck and smacked my lips. "I'm gonna eat you," I told her.

Rey's skin turned clammy and pale.

I wanted to tell her I often joked like an asshole, but kept my mouth shut. She should fear me. I had her fear and nothing else going for me. It would keep her within the city walls when I left for the day. She could take off on me like her sister took off on Benji before I had to put him out of his misery.

I caught Vice's gaze. He shook his head in disapproval.

Fuck him. Vice had courted his mate for weeks. Even before he'd claimed her, he broke our code and told his mate he couldn't have another. Said he'd give her the world. Little shit took off running the same night, and we hadn't caught her since. Ain't happening with mine. I tucked Rey closer.

Rey sipped her drink and covered her dislike of it with another of her fake smiles. I had to watch her. She covered up pretty well. I bet she was an excellent little liar. Came from a family of crooks.

At last, Rey put her glass down on the table.

Glasses clicked together.

Tchai spilled over my hand before the glass hit the floor. I gripped Rey's hips, planted my feet, and shoved the bench back about ten feet away. "Damn it!" I said. I'd almost dropped her.

"I'm sorry, I'm sorry," Rey said, frantically moving her hair over her shoulders. Her small feet crunched the glass as she ran back to the table. She took out tissues from her backpack and tried to clean up the mess.

What the hell? I stomped after her. "Don't run on the fucking glass."

"Okay," she said.

"Hey." I put my hand on her shoulder. "Let Karen clean up. Shit happens, don't worry about it." Tchai seeped through the thin tissues and drenched her fingers. Instead of swiping the tissue over the spill, Rey dabbed and dabbed and dabbed. "Watch out!" I shouted.

"Ah!" She jerked her hand away with a piece of glass stuck in the middle of her palm.

"Fuck. Me." I grabbed her wrist and turned her palm. "Let me see." *Motherfucker.* Should've just taken her home.

And of course, people gathered around us to see. I

spotted Karen, who stood at the table like she didn't have things to do. "Whatcha looking at?"

"It was an accident," Rey said.

"Nothing, she's a klutz," Karen answered me. She had a death wish too. "Watch your mouth," I said. "Vice? Didn't I say to tell her not to come around?"

"I told her."

"I'm no good anymore," Karen started. I knew what was coming. That little flavor called drama. The one I didn't want spoken in front of my mate. We, the beasts, loved to fuck. We fucked often, and we fucked hard. If unmated, we needed to get it like everyone else got it before they committed. Everyone had a history, and so did I, but I wanted to mate with Rey tonight, and I wanted to settle down. I didn't want her thinking anyone else mattered to me, because they didn't. But Karen always had a mouth too big for her health, and she didn't disappoint. "Well, well, well, aren't you two something? Alpha Beast, I didn't think you'd mind. A few weeks ago, you didn't mind. And you?"

She looked at Vice but didn't get a chance to say anything because I interrupted and said, "Bad shit happens when you think, because when you think, you're not thinking at all. Mind your position and your mouth. Vice, escort her outside the city."

Karen rested her hands on her hips. I shook my head when Vice grabbed her elbow to escort her out.

"Hey, get off me!" she shouted. "You'll tire of the Jamie act. That little whore won't know what to do with you."

I searched Rey's face for signs of jealousy, but she didn't seem to give a shit. Yeah? Well, she'd give a shit once she got used to her new life and me.

Man, of all the women on this planet, I got a sweet native mate. I needed a female bitch, and not this...this...

man, she was beautiful. I had to take care of her hand. My perfect girl might be clumsy, and that was okay with me, 'cause I wasn't.

A piece of glass stuck out of her palm. Blood trailed down the sides of her hand. She stared at it. I licked the blood from her hand. Sweet. "Don't listen to her," I said, even though she didn't give a shit. "Or anybody. You know how it is in the city." I plucked the glass from her palm, and she winced. "Nasty cut. Let's get it cleaned." I tugged her wrist and led her inside, where I sat her down on a soft, worn-out couch, then left to get the supplies.

# CHAPTER 4

*Rey*

Back inside the compound, I sat on a leather couch and fisted my hand. The cut burned and bled. I didn't expect the Alpha Beast to tend to it, but right in front of me, a chair scraped the floor and a black mass sat down. It could only be Jamie. None of the others were this big. How tall was he?

He took my hand in his. Although rough, his hands were tender; claws scraped my skin but didn't slice. As he poured—I sniffed—peroxide over the cut and wrapped gauze over my hand, I pretended to survey the surroundings while I really listened and inhaled the scents dominating the room. Since I'd lost my sight, my other senses had strengthened, and because I used to see before my accident, it was easy to paint a picture of the room.

To my left, the people chatted around the bar or at least a popular place where drinks got served. To my right, several voices followed footsteps. Coming and going, coming and going. Maybe the hallway to the bathrooms?

"Alpha Beast?" a soft, young female voice said.

"Not now," he said.

"The cake is ready."

"Enjoy."

"Um..."

"Mind?" he asked.

"What?"

"Um means mind in Tineyan."

"Um...You need to cut the cake."

"Says who?"

"Says Earth customs."

"No."

"I worked two days on that cake. Don't think for a second you won't be paying me for it because you won't cut it. I want my money."

"Who the fuck're you?" Jamie asked.

"Catering. Best Cake and Deco? You placed an order a week ago."

"Viiiiccccce!" he bellowed.

I gripped the couch so as not to jump out of my skin. Best Cake and Deco might lose their employee. Jamie's voice sounded like he'd eat her *and* her cake.

Vice's answer followed the springs creaking under his weight as he sat down next to me. "Great cake," he said. "I'm gonna have a sugar-coated bride. She looks delicious."

I chuckled and allowed myself to both blush and enjoy this stranger. Vice flirted. It'd been...never since men flirted with me. A wicked man.

"Pay her and get her out of here," Jamie said.

"But what do I do with the cake?" the girl asked.

"Bitch's holy pussy! Eat the cake, girl. Vice," Jamie growled, then took my arm. "We're going home, baby. Come on."

"I don't mind if we stay," I said.

"We're not staying."

"You could stay. I don't mind if you stay...alone, and do what you want. If you drop me off at our new home and return, I don't...don't mind."

Jamie's hands left me like I'd burned them. This time he didn't growl—he snarled.

I intertwined my fingers over my lap. Behind my sunglasses, my eyes blinked and blinked. A reflex, something they'd done ever since my accident. I hated that I couldn't stop it. I'd never been a coward, but I didn't want to lose anything else. Jamie might be a beast with a short fuse. I said nothing else. I only wanted to be left alone. I didn't want him to learn anything about me tonight.

---

*Jamie*

*Did she... What the fuck did she just tell me?* I'd cleaned up her hand and wrapped it the best I knew how. I wasn't a nurse. Should've let our healer handle her, but he'd strike up a convo with my mate and try to piss me off by flirting. So I took care of it myself.

I snarled.

Man, I'd been growling more than usual the past week. My peach must think I'm a damn hound. Fuck. A hound. I had to go back to her community for the damn hound. Well, nobody said mating between different species was easy.

I couldn't quite comprehend what she was trying to say to me. Oh, I comprehended, but I didn't wanna hear that shit from her.

But then my peach went on to explain, drill that shit into my head. Rey said, "I meant only for tonight or tomorrow before we...you know... If...if that's what you need. I'm tired."

On cue, the chatter in the room died.

Tired? Bullshit. "Tired," I repeated. I looked around at the room full of my male beasts, some mates, some native girls, some bitches—beast females—and all-around happy motherfuckers who couldn't wait to meet a woman who'd settle me down. Every one of them sported a sly grin, and everyone just loved to piss me off. Including my mate.

They'd heard our business. The business I wanted to explain to my peach a while from now and not tonight. She didn't get it. Fine. I'd show her our business. Right around the time when I shoved my cock into her pussy and told her she was mine. But seeing as she put me on the spot, I moved her sunglasses to rest on top of her head, then plastered my frame to hers so she could hear and understand me. "My beautiful girl," I said through my teeth. I palmed her hip. "The light of my days, the girl I can't get out of my head."

"Thank you," she said.

"Mm-hm. I am a happily paired man."

She relaxed into my hold. I liked that, but I wasn't done. I trailed a hand up her cheek and into her long hair, and lifted the one on her hip and landed it on her ass. Hard. Oomph, she stepped into me from the impact, bumping her big tits against my chest. My hand on her ass and the one in her hair tightened. I yanked her hair back and bit the base of her neck.

---

*Rey*

. . .

I yelped when he bit me, then pinched my lips together because the room was so damn quiet. Soft rock played low in the background. The room went silent of all chatter. Jamie's teeth dug in, and he growled so loud, my body vibrated. I found his shoulders and patted them. He was a big man, as wide as a fridge. I was better off not seeing him anyway; he'd probably make me wanna take off at a run. A blessing I couldn't see him. A bright side in the dark.

The patting must've worked, because he released my neck. "You are telling me," he said at my ear, "I should go and fuck another woman on my pairing night."

I wanted him to know I wasn't gonna begrudge his cheating. I couldn't even if I wanted to. I had to put up until I got away or died. I'd love to be the only one for him. Tonight, I wasn't prepared to be a wife just yet. He expected perfection. He expected babies. Even without thinking of running, I needed to get comfortable with my surroundings first. I didn't even know where the bathroom was, and I couldn't ask anyone or I'd be found out and returned. I couldn't have him return me. So, I thought a bit of communication in between our lies would do us some good. My mother was a whore. I knew how men worked.

"Yes, it won't offend me. Tonight." I didn't know why I added that last bit. Wishful thinking.

"And tomorrow night?" he asked.

"If that's what you want."

He spoke so low, I barely heard him. "You will pay for this offense." He bit my ear.

Sometimes it was best if I shut up. This turned out to be one of those times. I honestly didn't think I'd offend him.

How could I have offended him? Dad and his brothers fucked so many women, their wives didn't even call it cheating. Leslie called it sharing, and some others straight-out didn't even want their men around. In fact, they pretended it was normal, a part of their life, and if they made a fuss about it, they got placed in a home so far away from the main community house, they'd need a full tank of hydro-fuel to get to their man. Right now, I didn't want to be placed far from Jamie, the only person I knew around here. A man who dragged me around, which helped more than offended me.

"Rey, honey," Vice said and tugged my hand.

"Vice has a death wish," Jamie said and slapped his hand away. "You might have one too. Did you cut yourself on purpose so you'd go home?"

I stepped back. "No, of course not."

"You sure?"

"Yes, I'm damn sure."

"'Cause I know girls from your community do crazy shit to get attention and even crazier shit not to get any. Let me lay it out for you. I don't fall for it, been there and rode that crazy train with Vice. Let's get this straight. You are...all mine. If you don't wanna pair with me, just fucking say it, because I don't need to force myself on bitches. Bitches come all over me.

"I'm not trying to be a bitch," I mumbled.

Beasts around the bar snorted.

"A beast female is a bitch. It's your fucked-up community who misinterprets our culture. Another thing. If you got something to say to me, you tell me at home and not here. And even when you tell me shit at home, don't fucking tell me what to do."

"I didn't mean to—"

"Yes, you did. You think I bought you to put you at home so I can go whore around."

Okay, then. I shut up, didn't want to piss him off anymore.

"We're going home," he declared.

Jamie sounded like he wanted to be paired with me. I was his. Despite the way he'd delivered his possessive speech, I loved what he'd said. I'd never been anyone's.

# CHAPTER 5

*Rey*

One of Mom's many men slipped past her radar, and his greasy fingers slipped into my dry channel. It lasted only for a few nights. Later, he got bored, couldn't fit his big cock inside my small frame, and he didn't feel like putting an effort into it. A blessing. I was six years old.

At sixteen, I found a boy who wasn't scared of my dad, and I used him for sex. Following a great several months of fumbling, I got the hang of it, got pretty good at sex. It didn't last as long as I would have liked. At eighteen, I was too busy learning how to deal with sight loss. It'd been a while since I'd had sex. A blessing around the community.

In our bedroom, Jamie's hands slipped the sunglasses from my head. He lifted my white dress and threw it somewhere to his right. He turned me around and bent me over. I braced with my elbows on the bed. Underwear slid just below my ass cheeks, and he caressed my ass with his rough hands. "You're mine. Say it."

"I'm yours," I said.

"It means I'm yours." He slapped my ass.

I winced but didn't make a peep.

He slapped again.

*Again.*

*Again.*

I buried my face in the mattress.

"You will not even dream of telling me to go elsewhere. You will serve me in all things as pairs serve each other. Yes?"

*Again.*

I squeezed my eyes shut and let out a breath. "It hurts."

"It's supposed to. Believe me, it hurts me more."

*Again.*

I chewed the inside of my mouth.

*Again.*

"What did I say I'd do?"

"Um..."

"Mind?"

*Again.*

"I don't know!"

*Again.*

I tried to think while he spanked me. "Mount me? You said you'd mount me like a...a bitch."

"Is bitch a bad word around here?"

"It's a beast female."

"You hate that word," he said and squeezed my ass.

I opted for truth and said, "Yes." Oh, my ass hurt. I wanted to rub it but didn't dare put my hands there. He'd just spank me more.

"All right, peach. I'll remember things you don't like, while you should remember I keep my promises." He spat on his fingers and ran them through my slit. He said nothing else. He wasn't happy, and I wasn't happy I'd made him unhappy when I should've worked to make him ecstatic. If I knew how to suck him off right, I'd've choked on him, but I didn't, and making an idiot of myself wasn't on my agenda. Anymore. If he returned me, Uncle Sam would shoot me, so I enjoyed Jamie's attentions and continued on my mission to please him.

His fingers played over my entrance. They probed and withdrew, probed and withdrew. Heat pooled in my belly, and a soft moan escaped my lips. In response, he grunted, satisfied.

The head of his cock rested at my entrance. It pushed inside and stretched and stretched. It wanted to fit. Jamie's hand caressed my back, relaxed me, and I moaned louder, trying to accommodate his thickness. A large hand pressed the back of my neck and lowered my head to the bed.

"I ain't a gentleman. Maybe you've heard, maybe you didn't, but we're animals." He pushed into me, stretching me so wide, I thought I'd burst. A pause and he huffed out a breath. "Spread your legs a little more, and use your hands to open yourself."

I widened my stand and spread my ass cheeks. He pushed in some more. When would it end? His cock felt a foot long!

His fingers brushed my hip and trailed down to touch my clit. I gasped at the gentle rub of his fingers. He rewarded me with a pinch on my sensitive bud. "Your little pussy is tight and all mine. Say that it's mine."

"It's yours."

"You're gonna be a good girl for me, aren't you?"

"Yes."

"That's great, baby, now push back. Let your man inside." He slapped my clit.

"Oh!" I reared away from his hand and impaled myself to the hilt. I gasped, thought for sure I'd split in half. One hand on the back of my neck pressed my cheek to the mattress, and the other teased, slapped, and used my clit while he moved inside me. Slow and steady, he stretched me. My moans grew louder; his grunts followed. He yanked my hair back, my body arched off the bed, and he slapped my clit with rapid hits. I screamed my orgasm, but Jamie didn't stop.

He didn't even pick up his pace.

Slow and steady.

His mouth trailed over my neck.

My muscles relaxed, knees giving out, so I hooked my hand behind his neck to keep myself from falling. He placed his foot on the bed for better leverage and turned my face around so his tongue could push inside my mouth. I opened for him. He liked that and started pounding my pussy so hard, the bedframe banged on the wall, and when my legs shook, he spread his palm over my lower belly to hold me up in case the hand in my hair wasn't enough.

One last push and I felt him fill me.

He paused and breathed hard but didn't stop kissing me.

And he didn't fail to clean me up and tuck me into him after. "You're a champ," he said to me before my eyes closed. "I want to fuck every hole you've got, and that's what I'm gonna do. Get used to it. You gettin' used to it?"

I smiled in the dark and touched his face. My fingertips ran over his jaw first, and it was hard. His cheekbones next, and they were also hard, but his mouth was soft, and it turned up at the corners. When I got a good idea of what my husband looked like, I scooted closer and pressed my lips against his chest.

Jamie grunted and moved my hand into his hair. "Pet me." My smile widened as I ran my fingers through coarse hair that fell to his shoulders. I imagined Jamie had dark hair and piercing blue eyes. "Your people tell me..." he started, then rested his erection on my belly. Jamie's cock hadn't gone down. Oh my. "They tell me you like to cook, so I haven't gotten us anything. I'll take you to the marketplace...sometime midmorning, and you'll get what you want. I'll see my schedule tomorrow and call. Be ready, don't make me wait."

I'd rather he didn't. "If you'd give me a few days of space, that would be nice."

A claw hooked on the bottom of my chin and pushed my face up. "Space? You know that word you hate? I hate space the same way. I hate when you tell me you want space. What that tells me is that I'm invading your space as if it's a universe, and I'm a giant blob inside it. I've only had you for a half a night."

"I only meant I'd like to get around by myself for a while."

"You mean...independent of me?" He said "independent" as if spitting out a nasty bug. "Ever rode a bike?"

"No." Disaster!

"Then you depend on me, 'cause I gotta teach you how to ride in the city. Streets, buildings, how to land, where to go. What the fuck?"

"Only three days alone."

"No way."

My eyes watered. Tears threatened to spill. I blinked them back and hiccupped. Tomorrow was too soon.

"What is that? Are those tears?" He swiped a thumb under my eyes. Could he see in the dark? I was pretty sure we cuddled in a dark room.

Jamie put something in my hand. A tissue. *He sees in the dark.*

“Only three days?” he asked.

“Three.”

“A courting,” he declared. “For three days. You want me to court you.” A pause as he mulled it over. It took only a minute, and by the time he was done thinking about it, I felt like I'd been lying on pins and not a mattress. He pecked my lips. “The days are yours, babe.”

The nights were Jamie's.

## CHAPTER 6

### *Rey*

Midmorning, I sat up on the bed and listened. The house was quiet. "Jamie," I called out and waited. Nothing. He kept his promises. Excellent news, because I could explore and get a good feel for my new home. I needed to know where things were so I wouldn't trip over anything.

After the shower, I found a new dressing for my hand by the sink and replaced the old one with it. On my way downstairs, I counted the stairs of a three-bedroom town-home and came to a stop on the bottom floor. Hand stretched out in front of me, I counted my steps to a dark painting that hung against a white wall right across the stairs. I followed the hallway along the wall. It led me into a large room. I rounded the corner and hit a marble counter. This was the kitchen, and it was done in dark colors against white walls and floors. The contrast was a good thing.

Both hands running along the counter, I inspected it for electronics and objects, but mainly for the stovetop and the oven because those burned. I mentally marked the first corner, then a long workspace, then another corner where I found the coffeemaker and a toaster before a double-door fridge. The fridge fit into the third corner. A step away from the sink was a stovetop with an oven underneath.

A car zoomed above the house. I froze, hoping it wasn't Jamie. Did he own a car? When the car landed on the road with a soft hiss, I knew the kitchen window above the sink opened to the street. I waited for someone to come in, and wiped my sweaty palms on my shorts. After a while, when nobody showed up, I reached up and checked the window. The drawn blinds blocked the morning sunlight. And prying eyes. Good.

Next, I searched for a dining room table and found a bar island in the middle of the large kitchen. It had drawers underneath and barstools around it. I sat on the tall stool and tapped the bar's smooth metal surface. In the middle, I found a pen, a rectangular paper—probably a note—and what I thought was a stack of cash. On top of the note Jamie had left me was a small oval object. It had two buttons. Okay, then. I pressed one.

*Beep! Beep! Beep! Beeeeep!*

An alarm sounded.

I pressed the same button to shut it off.

It didn't shut off.

I leapt from the chair and got down on all fours with high hopes I wouldn't hit my head on the wall. All fours was better than tripping and injuring myself, so I scooted out of the kitchen, around the corner, and to the end of the hallway, where I threw my hand out and hit a smooth metal door. The front door. The car beeped behind it. I pressed the other button.

The car alarm kept beeping.

I pressed it again.

Nothing.

"The hell!"

I pressed both buttons.

The beeping ceased.

I exhaled a breath and leaned my forehead on the door.

Jamie had left me a car or a bike I couldn't drive. Jamie had left me a note I couldn't read. In the cities, they might have tech that could read things to me, but since we didn't have high tech in the communities, I wouldn't know where to look or how to use it. Another thing I needed Jamie to do for me. What could I do for him before I asked him a million and one things I needed to become independent? Could I get out of here on my own? I could. I'd figure it out.

First thing first. He wanted to taste my cooking. It would buy me a good day with him. I crawled back into the kitchen and opened the fridge. There had to be some eggs. Everyone had eggs. My fingertips ran over a pitcher of—I sniffed—tchai, lots of beer bottles, and one plastic box—I opened to sniff—food. Hungry, I took the food.

Scrambling from the floor, I found a drawer with cutlery and got a fork. White cake frosting melted on my tongue. Our wedding cake. Someone must've dropped it off this morning. Closing the fridge, I sat on the floor and leaned my back against it. I dug into my breakfast of champions. The not-vanilla cake was fluffy and delicious, the frosting sweet on my tongue.

"Good morning, house," I said. "You and I will need to

be friends, or I might burn you down by accident. Can you start a cup of coffee for me? No? Well, that sucks."

Twenty bucks said the note left instructions on how to use the beeping vehicle to get to the marketplace, where I'd use the money to buy whatever I needed. I chuckled.

*Drip. Drip. Drip.*

Fork poised halfway to my mouth, I froze. "Who's there?"

*Drip. Drip. Drip.*

Coffee. I sniffed again. Someone just turned the coffeemaker on, which meant someone was in the kitchen with me. I scrambled away and into the corner, and when Uncle Sam swung a pitchfork at my head, I covered it with my hands.

I rocked.

It wasn't real.

He wasn't real, but behind my eyes, I saw memories. When I was frightened, Uncle Sam swinging the pitchfork at me came as a flashback. I rocked some more because the scene would pass. "Who's there?" I peeked between my elbows. I didn't see or hear anyone. Okay, okay, I needed to cool my shit. Jamie had said he had a cat. Perhaps his cat climbed the counter and pressed the button to start a cup of coffee? "Kitty!" I called out.

By the time Jamie phoned later in the afternoon, the house and I had gotten to know each other pretty well. I'd tripped only once on the cat's little toy mouse, but hadn't found the cat. Maybe the cat was an outdoor type and preferred to run around the neighborhood. Just as well, because I'd called it several times while searching for cat food. No cat, but I found a bag of food.

"How's a day in your space goin'?" Jamie asked as I sat down on the new leather couch in the living room. This entire home smelled new. Even the wall paint.

Jamie was bitter about space. "Great. Yours?" I'd much rather he told me about his day.

"You like your spacious house?" he asked.

"I love it."

"Did you get to the market yet? It's a space station away."

"You're being a big baby," I said.

He chuckled. "I need razors, and I forgot to get you a toothbrush."

"I brought mine so... And I have extra razors too."

"Those little pink disposable things?"

"They're purple." Weren't they purple?

"A man razor, baby. I ain't using pink or purple shit. Get me MachoBeast number three, would you? Don't cook on the first day, I'll get us pizza on the way back. Did you figure out the appliances? I left you a note."

"Okay," I said. "Macho three."

Silence descended. I waited because I didn't know what to say. The Alpha Beast was not the man I'd expected him to be. He seemed to care. He could've bought any girl, I reminded myself.

"I also left you something on my nightstand. Was gonna give it to you yesterday, but changed my mind and thought it'd be a nice surprise when you woke up today. All alone in your space. Did you see it?"

I stood and counted the steps to the stairs. There were two staircases. Home phone at my ear, I climbed the seven steps of the first staircase, rounded the corner, and climbed up and up the step before the last.

"Meow." The cat announced her presence.

Too late.

I tripped and tumbled down both flights of stairs, losing the phone in the process. The back of my head hit the wall. I winced when I bounced off and hit my forehead on a glass door. It shook. I immediately covered my head in case the glass shattered.

The shaking settled. *Oh, thank God.*

Heat rushed into my cheeks, and a small bump formed on my forehead. I tapped it. Not bad. It'd be fine, and I hadn't broken anything, including the glass, which I was pretty sure was the back door leading to our backyard.

Still, I stayed down for a bit. The side of my thigh hurt, and I rubbed it.

"Rey!" Jamie shouted from the phone.

I got back on all fours and followed his voice. "I dropped the phone! Hold on." Where was the damn phone?

"Rey, I'm coming!"

Frantic, I hurried back up, tapping the stairs with both hands, careful not to hit the poor cat again.

"Re—"

The cat answered him with a mew.

My hand landed on a smooth oval object. "Found it!" I announced and pressed the phone against my ear with my shoulder while crawling the rest of the stairs to the top and into our bedroom.

"You all right?" Jamie asked.

"Oh, just a phone accident. Don't worry about it. What's your cat's name?"

"Our cat," he corrected. "And I haven't named it yet."

"Is it a girl?"

"Got big balls, so no."

"Light," I said, thinking about my hound, Dark. I tapped the nightstand and found the object he'd left me.

"Light it is. Are you upstairs yet?"

"Yes, mm-hm." On the floor, I leaned my back against the bed, fingers playing with a small velvet box.

"Open it," he said.

I did. Inside, my fingertips felt a pair of rings. One solid and the other with a large round stone pointing up. My hand flew to my mouth when a sob threatened to escape. I dropped the box with the rings. Rings were our customs, not theirs. This was for me.

"Do you like them?"

I took a few seconds to calm down, and then I said, "They're beautiful."

"That's sweet, baby. Your little voice makes me very hard, so I gotta go talk with some of these fuckers here and get my boner down. But don't worry, I'm gonna dip into your sweet peach tonight. And the night after for the rest of my life. What do you say?"

"Yes, Jamie."

We hung up, and I placed the box back on the nightstand. Then I found my pills in the wooden box I'd brought in my pack. I took a few to get back on the bright side of life. I wasn't one to wallow in self-pity, but I also didn't refuse chill pills on days I knew I couldn't find the bright side. My heart ate at me for lying, but my brain told me to hold on for a few more days, until I had a backup plan in case Jamie decided he didn't want to be paired anymore. Despite the rings promising me forever, it could happen. Anything could happen. My great-grandparents didn't believe in aliens, but here they were. My eyesight was fine for eighteen years. And now it wasn't. Anything could happen, and I'd learned that lesson the hard way.

Life was a dealer. Some people got a shitty hand, but I always hoped the next hand it dealt me would hold my wild card. Maybe Jamie was my wild card, and if so, I had to use the card wisely, even if I felt like shit for doing it.

The pills helped me deal, and I napped for hours, effectively sleeping the day away.

I forgot to put the rings on my finger.

When Jamie came home, he threw the box against the wall, then closed the bedroom door. I pretended to sleep.

Around midnight, I crawled in search of my rings. I slipped them on and cried quietly, listening to the TV downstairs.

# CHAPTER 7

*Jamie*

"Da fuck you mean the hound ain't there?" I growled into the phone, already straddling my bike. I whistled and jerked my head. Vice understood we were gonna take a little ride back to my mate's uncle. "You better tell me you'll find the damn thing by the time I get there."

"Can't do," he said.

"You *will* do."

"Can't. Someone already took the hound. Swiped it right as you took up into the sky."

"Who?"

"Don't know her."

"Her? It was a woman?"

"From Community Three."

I put him on speaker as Vice approached. "I thought you said you didn't know her."

"Community Three. That's all I know. Saw her. Dark

skin, fiery-red hair to her ass. Jumped down from her car before it landed. Hydro-skater I think."

Vice froze in place. I knew he thought it was Dewlyn, his mate. Hell, we both knew it had to be Dewlyn. Community Three's girls had dark skin and fiery hair, and Dewlyn skated over skyscrapers. Crazy hair to match the crazy under the hair if you asked me, but I tried not to judge my sister-in-law, the girl who'd left my brother when he'd laid out his cards. Dewlyn had said ugly things to him. There was nothing he could do about it but run after her. Such was mating. One-sided. Same as mine.

I'd never tell Rey anything. A day and a half of fucking space to go. I flexed my claws as if preparing for battle. Space? My mate already got her space. She struggled with her new life, and I didn't know what to do when she didn't want me to do anything. Fuck forbid Rey left me the same way. I shuddered. With the rings back on the nightstand, the future smirked at us.

Hanging up the phone, I locked eyes with Vice's red ones.

"She's been following me," Vice said. "What does she want with the hound?"

"If she followed us, she saw the owner. She'll talk to my mate is what she's gonna do."

"I'll handle it," Vice said.

I didn't believe him but nodded anyway.

We started up the bikes. They lifted off the ground, and the tires folded. I revved the engine and propelled us to our houses, where we set up a lookout on top of a far building.

Mine and Vice's homes sat on one side of the road, and the neighborhood was on the other. We were born predators, and my eyes glowed bright silver as I surveyed every person in my field of vision. "She knows where Rey is.

When she knocks on my door, Rey's gonna let her in," I said.

"She might not."

"She will."

"How do you know?"

"Because I know. Let Dewlyn drop off the hound. We'll get her when she goes inside the house. I'll put the house on lockdown, and you take her. Nice and quiet. This is a family neighborhood, remember? There are kids and fucking curly haired poodle hounds. Let's not make drama."

"Your new hound will fit right in with the poodles," Vice said.

I slapped my brother's back. "That hound's gonna bang his way through the poodle pack."

"How's Rey?"

"Didn't want the rings."

"Keep at it," Vice said. "Be nice."

"I'm a peach, and I'm courting her. Every day I leave her a toy on the nightstand. We're gonna try my new toy tonight. She'll like it."

"What is it?"

"Anal hook."

"Peachy. Does she even know what it is?"

"Doubt it, but she will tonight."

"Let me give you a tip," Vice started, and I rolled my eyes, bored already. "There are still, oooo, maybe eighty percent of people on this planet who don't know how we roll. Maybe Rey's one of them."

"She'll get used to it."

"You're going about it all wrong, bro."

"Too soon?" I nodded in agreement. "How would you court her?"

"I'd go for the anal plug."

*Rey*

"Hey, you," I said to Jamie's cat, Light, who ate my hair. Lots of hair to chew on. My great-grandmother was Greek, and I inherited volumes of long, dark brown curls. From my dad, Don, from Ireland, I inherited green eyes. Small waist, long legs with a big ass and big breasts. I knew why Jamie had paired with me at first glance.

I threaded my fingers through the cat's soft fur. He purred. And continued to purr for a while since I had nothing else to do but pet the animal and allow it to chew my hair. We were friends already. So much for escaping this house. I couldn't even make it outside, too scared of the city I'd never seen before. When had I become such a coward?

The phone rang.

"Hello," I answered.

"Rey of the Alpha Beast?" a woman asked.

"Yes?"

"Did you lose a hound?"

Abruptly, I sat up. The cat protested with a hiss. "I lost my hound the day before yesterday. Do you have him?" Hope blossomed in my chest. Someone had found him.

At the sound of my voice, Dark barked in the background. My heart swelled.

"What kind of a hound is it?" the woman asked.

She wanted an ID. "A gray hound." At least my mother had described him as such. "He's got a patch of black on his belly and answers to Dark. Got a thick black leather collar with a purple tag."

"Got your hound, girlfriend. Yay!"

"Yay!" I repeated.

"So, you wanna get him? He looked hungry and tired, and I gave him a Fast-Kid's meal on my way back from work. Is ham okay? He's riding in my car. I'm heading home."

I didn't recognize the young woman's voice, so she wasn't from my community, which was the nearest community to the Beast City. Dark must've snuck into another community.

All right. I sighed, thinking. Two problems. I couldn't get him all the way from her community, and Jamie didn't want a hound in the house. If I told him I needed Dark, I'd need to explain why I needed him. One night of great sex followed by a disastrous night where he'd slept on the couch did not a pairing make. Returning me back to Uncle Sam wasn't an option.

Screw Uncle Sam.

Screw Jamie too.

The Alpha Beast had signed the pairing without even meeting me. He shouldn't have, but he had. A done deal, and there was nothing I could do to change that. Jamie had signed up for a life with me. He should've asked to meet with me first!

Terrified he'd find me a burden the way Uncle Sam and even my mom had after my "accident," I needed to find a way to preserve our pairing for a bit longer until I found a way out. Or until he saw me for me and not for the long, dark hair and tight pussy. Looks were superficial. Pounding a pussy for sex's sake wasn't gonna keep him coming home to me either. I was fairly certain Jamie was handsome, and even if he wasn't, the power he carried probably got him laid more often than I'd like to know. I felt terrible for leading him on, but I had to take care of myself. Nobody else would take care if I didn't.

I couldn't go back to the community. My dad was dead. My mom was dead. Uncle Sam would get rid of me. People wouldn't even notice I was gone.

"You still there?" the woman asked.

I swallowed my troubles, refocused on the now. I needed someone to show me around, and then I could do everything on my own. Dark would show me around. "Sorry, yes. Which community is yours? I'll get him by tomorrow. I've moved, and my car is...is in the shop for the day."

"Oh, that's not a problem. I found him in the City, right by the Beast's main compound."

"He followed the bikes from the community," I whispered in disbelief. "That's a hundred plus miles. My poor baby, his paws must be raw."

"Very cool hound, huh?"

Dark barked in confirmation. He was cool.

"He deserved his Fast-Kid meal. I'll pay you back for it. Thanks so much, he means the world to me." Happy tears spilled, and I let them. How could I get him? I wiped my face and sniffed. "Where do you live?"

"Let's meet at the City Park."

"I'm new in the area, and I don't know where that is, but if you give me—"

"I'll come by."

*Click.*

"Hello?"

No answer.

I pressed the touch screen. Things beeped. I presumed I'd pressed buttons, so I tried to find a redial one.

*Beep.*

She hadn't taken my address. I didn't even know my address. "What is my house address?" I mumbled.

"House of the Alpha Beast. House Nine, Street E, Zone One of Beast City," a female voice said.

I placed my hand over my collar and gripped the little heart pendant. "Oh dear God, what is that? Who are you?"

"I. Am. House Nine. Street E. Zone One of Beast City."

The house spoke! "Hello, House Nine. I'm Rey."

"Hello, Rey. Would you like a cup of coffee?"

"Yes, oooh yes." I even clapped my hands at the tech. "But first, how can I redial a number?"

"Press the green button."

"Thank you. Very useful. I cannot see the green button. I do not see any buttons. Is it on the top or the bottom?" I ran my fingertips over the touch screen and, presumably, the numerous buttons. Things around the house beeped. Was this even the phone or a controller? "Hopefully, the button's not in the middle," I said.

"Processing Rey's replies. Please wait."

A minute later, I fidgeted in my seat, seeing as I'd lost the sense of urgency with the woman on the phone. I bit my nail. "Are you done processing?"

"Yes. Voice commands are activated on all appliances. Speak into the appliance."

Phone in hand, I touched my lips to the phone. "Hello. Phone."

Nothing happened. "It's not working," I announced. The house didn't reply. "Hellooo. House?"

"Yes, Rey?"

Okay, okay. So to address the house, I had to say "house." "House, I don't understand how you work."

"I do not work."

"Operate!"

"Processing. Please wait."

Damn it!

*Drip. Drip. Drip.*

The house processed the coffee. I'd play nice with the house and wait until it processed. I bit my other fingernail. Once done, House mimicked my voice and said, "Command redial."

Well, hearing my own voice was a bit freaky, but the phone redialed and rang on the other side.

"House, can you use Jamie's voice?"

"Who is Jamie?"

"Alpha Beast."

"Yes, Rey," the House said in his deep baritone. I smiled and waited for the woman to answer. I'd get Dark. Somehow. What I'd do with Dark after he got here, I'd worry about it after he was here.

Minutes later, I couldn't get the woman back on the phone. I thought about the pills but poured a cup of coffee instead.

## CHAPTER 8

### *Rey*

An hour later, unable to get in touch of the woman and get Dark back, unable to make anything for dinner because I didn't have any food, memories of Mom assaulted me. I didn't want to have another bad day. I tried to force my brain to think about the memories I wanted to embrace in favor of the ones I wanted to forget. I wanted to remember my mom as the good mom she could've been. After she'd overdosed, I couldn't shake off the guilt that rode me when I thought about her. I only remembered her bad days. And they were many.

Sitting on the floor, I leaned my back against the couch. Mom tried to stay sober when I'd lost my sight. She'd tried. At least I liked to think she'd stayed away from drugs and alcohol. I wanted to treat her addictions as a disease. I wanted not to blame her and feel guilty about blaming her. But it was hard to treat an addiction as a disease when I knew it was one she could've cured with willpower. When did lack of willpower become a disease? And when were people better people once they'd died? Did death make people better, somehow justified the way they'd lived and what they'd done while alive?

I asked the House to recite me all its functions.

In Jamie's voice.

It soothed me, cleansed away the ugly thoughts. When more memories drifted through my mind, I cringed, not wanting to think about the day Uncle Sam came to fuck Mom and found me sleeping in her bed. He'd said things I was too young to understand. I understood them later when it was too late.

Not remembering wasn't working for me today. I crawled to the fridge for more of my pairing cake. Before I ate everything, I saved one piece for Jamie, then dug in at the table, stuffing my mouth with happy thoughts. I thought about him and his warm body against mine, and I thought about his mouth and his big hands, and how I didn't want to experience his disappointment. I knew he'd be disappointed because Jamie had bought a perfect peach.

A peach who didn't even dare to go out and walk in the backyard.

Not even with a cane.

But I had to get out, or I'd rot in the house, fall back into the depression hole I'd crawled out of last year. Dealing with sight loss and Mom's drinking and drug use took a long time. Dad didn't really know what to do with me. Not that he made the time to do anything with me either.

I wiped my face and breathed deep, sat there for a while.

I needed to get some fresh air.

A knock sounded at the front door. On the other side of the door, Dark barked, announcing his presence. I nearly tripped over my feet to answer. I flung the door open, a big grin on my face. "My boy!" Dark tried to curb his excitement and went to work immediately. He placed his body next to my leg and waited for the leash, but his rapid tail wagging shook his whole body and gave him away. He didn't want to work. He wanted to play. "Thank you," I said to the silhouette against the sunlight as I knelt to pet Dark. "Oh, I am so glad you came by." Not that I'd given her an address or anything, but maybe she had tech to find my address.

I frowned. How did she even know my phone number? A cold shiver ran down my spine. I'd answered the door for a stranger. It didn't matter she was a woman. I shouldn't have flung it open the way I had. I looked up. "Hello? Anyone?" Nobody was there. I squinted against the daylight and tried to pick up on dark masses on the street. There weren't any.

I guessed the girl had left without a word, so I closed and locked the door behind me. Bending, I hugged Dark and inhaled his hound scent. I scrunched up my nose. I'd need to give him a bath, but first I checked his paws since he'd run for hours. When I pressed on the soft bottoms, he didn't respond or jerk his paw away as if in pain. I ran my fingertips over the bottoms of the paws and didn't feel any cuts or objects imbedded inside. "You're not even sore," I told him. Weird, but okay. "Here's what we'll do. We'll find you a place in the backyard so Jamie doesn't go crazy and bite you. Don't tell him I said that. Then we'll rest. Do you like cats?"

Dark barked a definite yes. Or so I told myself.

Neither Dark nor I were ever trained on guidance. We trained together, worked together the best we could. At first, when I'd found him outside the community gates, we fumbled a lot. Back then, depressed and angry at the whole world, I often contemplated whether life was worth living. Dark taught me more about sight and humanity than any other person I knew. When he first started to lead me around by barking, I got out of my self-pity stage and rushed head-on to train with him. Although Dark had failed the temperament training once, he was a smart animal and, to be honest, a pretty good judge of character. He hated Uncle Sam and had bitten him.

I reached for Dark's leash. He whined, in a way telling me I'd taken it off in the community. "I'm sorry, boy. I didn't have a choice, but I promise I'll work on the big bad beast." I needed to leash Dark, hold him next to me, so we could go out in the backyard and he could see where I stepped. I had to find a place to hide him for the night, and I wanted fresh air.

We went up to the bedroom while I spoke to Dark and told him about our new talking house. I wasn't crazy, I knew he didn't understand me, but when this animal was all I had for company, it wasn't crazy to speak to him. It would drive me crazy not to speak to anyone. In the past, a living, breathing animal in the house had been my salvation on days when all I had to look forward to were my soft footsteps in a dark house.

Upstairs, I dug into Jamie's side of the walk-in closet and found his drawers. I opened every one of them, then touched in between the racks of jeans and leathers. He must have old belts, Dad had a dozen belts. I tapped around and tapped some more. I didn't find a belt, and I knew I was running out of time. He'd be home any moment.

Dark nudged my leg.

I touched his head and his jaw. Something round, long, and coarse brushed my fingertips. It wasn't a belt. What was it? I gripped it and frowned, ran my hand over the long, flexible object. It was coarse yet not abrasive at the same time. “I think it’s rope.” Dark held Jamie’s rope between his teeth. A rope. In the bedroom. Okay, then.

I padded my way to Jamie’s side of the bed and placed my hand on top of the nightstand. Dark must’ve found it on the nightstand, because he couldn’t open the drawers. Patting the surface, carefully, so I wouldn’t knock things off, I knocked something off anyway. Quickly, I grabbed it before it fell.

I gripped a long, smooth, metal object. It curved like a fishhook with a ball on the tip. Jamie had left the rings on the nightstand too. A courting custom of a sort for him. This was another gift for me, but I had no idea what this was, so I placed it back on the stand.

Sighing, I threaded the rope through the metal hook of Dark’s collar and headed downstairs. I paused on the last step. I loved bikes. The entire neighborhood heard a man coming home.

I swung open the back door.

Dark went outside.

I crawled back upstairs.

# CHAPTER 9

*Jamie*

Rey had about three minutes to straighten up the things before I walked inside. We'd play a little interrogation game. The one where I asked questions and she answered. Like how in the world did she know Dewlyn? Had Dewlyn been in contact with her? What were they up to? Running together. My claws flexed.

In the driveway, I checked the bike to see if she'd used it. I'd programed it to city limits only, and the mileage read "sixteen." Same as yesterday. I stormed inside and sniffed out Rey, coffee, and a dirty hound. She'd hidden him somewhere thinking I wouldn't let her have it. And that was fine by me.

I whistled. My cat didn't come begging for food. Big Balls—Light was a better name—was fed and hiding from the hound. The smell of coffee told me she'd figured out how to use the house tech. Still, she hadn't gone to the marketplace. I opened the fridge and scouted the empty shelves. She ate only cake. Left me a piece. Coffee and cake. All she was eating. What the hell? Was she starving herself?

I slammed the fridge closed and walked to the glass door overlooking the backyard, where a hound sprawled in my damn lounge chair. He didn't even bother to turn and look at me. His tongue hung out of his drooling mouth, saliva pooling on my brand-new chair. Little shit. Hand on the door, I almost opened it, then decided I'd let her explain. I'd given her enough space. Two nights, and one of those nights I'd spent on my couch. Fuck space.

Three steps at a time, I climbed upstairs. I opened and closed the bedroom door, intended to speak with her about her damn space. I was gonna give her a piece of my mind. Inside a dark room, I threw the keys on the dresser and went to turn the lights on, thinking she pretended to sleep again.

And then I saw her. Naked. She knelt on the edge of the mattress and pressed her cheek to the soft cotton sheets, effectively giving me her ass and a slit between her legs. Her hair fanned out around her like a veil. Reaching under with little fingers, she teased her clit.

I stood behind her ass and looked down at her pussy, my mortal enemy. I inhaled. Man, if I had nipple clamps for her tits, I'd close them over my nose right now. I inhaled her budding arousal again. My claws flexed, and I grunted when my cock sprang up. "What's this?"

"A peace offering," she said.

"Damn straight."

She chuckled.

What happened to the piece of my mind I was gonna give her? My mate's peach pussy happened. I looked down at my erection. She had me by the balls. The mating worked its magic. It was as if Rey had said *Here's some sweet pussy, beasty boy,* and I said, *Yes, ma'am, gimme a lick.* What the fuck? I groaned and sat next to her. Leaning, I kissed one ass cheek, then kicked off my boots and undressed. After I walked around the bed, I took her hand and thumbed my rings. "You decided you liked the rock after all."

"I love it," she said. "I'm sorry about last night."

Damn straight. I glanced at the nightstand for the toys I'd left her. I wanted her to get familiar with things I wanted to do. "Baby, did you find my note downstairs?"

"Um, no, I didn't see it."

"It was on the bar." She didn't reply. "It's all right, maybe the cat played with it." The cat didn't play with it. The cat knew better than to climb my new kitchen.

"What did it say?" she asked.

"It said you should wear your butt plug tonight," I lied. "I left it here for you." I'd left rope and an anal hook.

"Ah yes. I didn't know what it was." A pause. "And there was no lube," she added.

"The lube's in the drawer." I'd teach her the difference between a hook and a plug soon. "Have you seen what's in the drawers?" I put the hook back in the drawer and got the plug. I lubed it and put in on the nightstand.

"I didn't want to...invade your side. For privacy, you know."

"Fuck privacy. I want you to learn what I like so that when I shove things up your ass, you'll know what's coming."

She chuckled. "I get it."

"Good. You got a hairbrush? A thick, strong one?"

Rey left for the bathroom while I searched under the bed for my rope. She returned with a wooden hairbrush and scurried back on the bed. I stuck my hand out and caught her hip to plop her on my lap. Her hair smelled like my shampoo. I didn't like it, and I didn't like how she often hung her head, rarely ever met my eyes. I turned up her face. Rey's body stiffened. "Look at me," I told her.

We locked eyes, and I heard her pulse pick up. Good. My mate had pretty green eyes framed in long eyelashes. She really was the most beautiful girl, and I couldn't be mad at her for five seconds, let alone five minutes. Still, I had to be firm so she knew I wasn't playing around. "Tonight, I'm gonna groom you and play with your ass and your pussy."

"Groom me?"

"Brush and braid your hair. Tomorrow is a new day. You can look forward to spending some more time with me, seeing as the space I've given you is too spacious. I'm worried about you. I know you take meds."

She hung her head again. "It was only yesterday. I don't take them every day."

"Who gave them to you?"

"My aunt."

I'd have a word with her aunt. Rey was twenty-one to my two hundred, and she wouldn't age anymore, because that was how mating worked. She was very young. At her age, I thought I knew everything about life when I didn't know shit. Under my claw on her chin, her jaw moved as she ground her teeth. Was she gonna bare her teeth at me? Oh, fuck that. I bared mine. She didn't flinch, but her heart beat faster.

Hm. Maybe scaring her wasn't such a good strategy. I contemplated this. A beast bitch would want to be scared, chased, and hunted, then impaled and fucked hard. Rey was no bitch. I had to figure this out on my own since I couldn't take much advice from my unwise brother. His mate ran around the land like a stray puppy.

"Back on Tineya, when I was twenty-one," I began, "I'd just finished my military training and I was ready to explore...space. My parents didn't let me, and I didn't like how they had control over what I did and didn't do. Dad and I butted heads for a year. One day, he sat me down and told me Tineya can't have more than one Alpha. So he gave me a ship and told me to get the fuck off his planet. Me, Vice, and Goner started planning our trip to Earth, and when we mapped our voyage, we took volunteers with us. You all needed some governing anyway, so we took over what was left of your cities."

"Who is Goner?"

"Goner is my younger brother. He crashed and burned. I renamed him Goner after. It's what my people do. We rename the dead."

She swallowed. "It fits."

"Took up Wolf for myself just in case. Remember that." The scent of her arousal drove me nuts. My hand found its way between her legs, and I played with her pussy lips while waiting for her to tell me it fit. Cold silver eyes Vice had said fit the name Wolf. Rey didn't say anything.

"And Vice?" She blushed a little.

"Why you interested in Vice? Because he kissed your hand? I'm gonna cut his hand off and gag his big mouth." I moved her to the bed and arranged her just the way I wanted her, kneeling with her back to me. I placed her palms on her thighs and stood behind her to watch her hair tickle her ass.

She showed me her profile. "I'm not interested in him."

"So why are you blushing?"

"Because..." She cleared her throat, clearly uncomfortable, but I wanted her to get on with it. She was mine, and she ought to fucking tell me everything. "I want to touch you too," she said.

Huh. There I unloaded my history thinking I'd get her

to unload some of hers, and all my peach wanted was to mate. I could do that, and I would after I cleared some air. She had me by the balls, and I'd have her by the pussy.

She wanted to stroke my cock. "Great, baby. Keep talking. I like this." I got the plug. One hand on her shoulder, I said at her ear, "I'll let you play with my cock, let your little hand slide up and down while your pouty little mouth sucks on it. Sit up a little." When she did, I pressed the tip of the plug to her asshole. "Now, sit down. Slowly, let it slide in." I pressed her shoulder and guided her down. The plug was seated, and Rey sighed in discomfort. It was okay. First time. It shouldn't be comfortable.

But I could make it comfortable. I poked her pussy with my finger, conscious of my claws. It was wet, and my finger glided in and out with ease. My peach needed attention; her greedy pussy told me so. "Does your pussy hurt like it's missing something?"

"Yes, it aches." She lifted her ass off her heels and lowered it to the mattress, trying to get more of my finger inside. I hovered on the outside and teased her. "Greedy little pussy," I said. "Wants something bigger. Your beast gonna give you bigger." I bit her ear. "You think you'd gag on me? I bet you would. Should I make you gag?"

She nodded, still trying to ride my finger, so I gave her two. I let her fuck herself, coat my fingers. When she got close to coming, and even though I loved hearing her come undone for me, I licked my wet fingers.

Rey protested.

I ignored her and picked up the hairbrush, spun it in my hand. Groom her hair or paddle her ass with it? Decisions, decisions. I opted for paddling because she kept trying to play with herself. Her fingers were back down there, and she rode them.

"Did you get your pussy nice and wet?" I asked.

"Mm-hm."

"Get your fingers out of there and put your hands here." I tapped the mattress, and she stretched her arms, hands folded on top of one another exactly where I'd tapped. She wiggled her ass while I shuffled through the drawers looking for my rope. "Where the fuck is my rope? Lock the bedroom from now on, I don't want animals in here." The cat might've chewed and clawed my rope, thinking it was his toy. Now I had a hound too. Definitely locking this room.

No rope meant I'd work with my hands and she'd have to do as told. Fine. One-handed, I took her wrists and placed them at the small of her back. I dropped to my knees so I could take a better look at her pussy. Rey's pussy was pink and small. Cute. "Baby," I said, and she startled at my breath on her wetness. "I'm gonna paddle your ass, okay?" She had a big ass. It would bounce and bounce, and I'd lick her like a puppy after. I ran my tongue over my canines.

"Um...if that's what you want."

"I want, and you will tell me if you don't like it. Yes?"

"Yes."

"You will not lie to me."

"Okay, Jamie."

I swung the paddle.

Rey yelped and immediately tried to get away. I held her down with my other hand and hit again. And again.

*Again.*

*Again.*

And over her pussy.

Rey screamed. Her pussy swelled, and I poked it with my tongue, sucked her clit between my teeth until she calmed, thinking I was done. I hit both cheeks real fast. *Snap, snap, snap, snap.*

Rey wiggled, then twisted to the side.

Two more.

I swung and hit the back of her thigh. My eyes glowed with excitement, watching her in pain. I tasted her pussy again, just a small lick so that I was sure she liked it. Her arousal filled the room. I swung one last time and placed the brush next to my knee.

Rey heaved breaths, probably relieved the paddling was over.

"What do you say?" I asked.

"Thank you?"

"Welcome. Scoot back closer," I said and grabbed her hips. I dragged her to the edge of the bed so she lay belly down on the mattress, with her knees spread and almost touching the floor, her red ass and peachy-sweet pussy in my face. I scooted back a little to get a better look. "Have you ever tasted your pussy?"

"Maybe."

"Good girl. Girls taste their pussies. They don't wanna admit it because that's dirty. Are you dirty?"

"Only in mind."

Gotta watch out for the quiet ones. Quiet girls spun dirty thoughts. "As long as your mind is filthy, your pussy will remain clean. It's a weapon, so I know whatcha doin'. We got problems, and you wanna distract me, don't you?"

"Of course not."

"Mm-hm. You know I want it, so you give it to me. Don't lie. What's your pussy taste like?"

Rey didn't answer.

I sucked her clit. Hard.

"Oh dear, oh, oh, it...it tastes like the fresh soap you use. Your soap, I use your soap, your everything. Yes, Jamie, oh yes." She reached behind her and gripped my hair.

I grunted into her pussy.

Rey squeaked.

Hm.

She spread her legs more, yanked my hair, and pushed back against my mouth, stuffing my face with her juices. What the fuck? Mortal enemy. I needed to conquer this one. So I did. I pressed my mouth to her and sucked the swollen bud. Then I inhaled its sweetness and let out a growl from the bottom of my chest.

Rey's back arched.

I smirked, still licking her.

I growled and spread her ass cheeks. I flicked her bud rapidly with the tip of my tongue. My tongue wasn't smooth like hers, it was rougher because I had better taste buds than the natives. I poked her pussy with it.

"Oh dear God."

When I had my tongue inside her, I snarled, letting my tongue vibrate against her walls. Rey's pussy fluttered, a butterfly to my beast, and she screamed her orgasm. Her chest rose up and down, her hair a mess around her face. I gave her a minute, ran a hand down her back, and licked my canines. I massaged the backs of her thighs. Her knees gave out, and she slid down to the floor with me, her ass right between my legs. Her back warmed my front, so I arranged her again how I wanted to mount her.

I locked her body between my knees. She braced her hands on the edge of the bed and leaned toward it, already knowing how I liked to fuck. This was good. Beaded with sweat, her back rose up and down as she breathed. I licked her shoulder and slowly removed her plug to replace it with my cock. Rey didn't protest. She rested her cheek on the mattress, closed her eyes, and sighed. I wanted her to be putty in my hands, relaxed and aroused and mad about me.

I wanted her to want me the way I wanted her. I was crazy about her.

When her shoulders slouched and her breaths evened, I slid slowly in and out of her ass. To get her mind away from the pain when my cock stretched her hole, I started braiding her hair. "You've not bought anything for yourself. I left you money, and it's still there. We got money, baby, buy whatever you want. You don't have to sit at home all day. Take the bike, go places. The day is yours. What's the matter? You miss home?"

She took her tits into her hands. Her tits were big, her hands small, so I helped her, brought her back to my front and moved her head to rest the back of it on my shoulder. She braced her hands on my thighs and nestled on my cock. I pushed forward with my hips while kneading her titties. I pinched her nipples.

"I don't miss home," she said between my slow thrusts. "I like it here."

"You don't know how to cook, is that it? They lied to me, said you owned your shit in the kitchen. I don't mind, but I wanna know if your uncle lied to me so he'd rip more money from me. I fucking hate when people are lying to me." I picked up my pace, gripped her collar. "Baby, are you lying to me?"

Rey said nothing.

I reached around her and teased her clit.

Her hand found mine, and we teased it together.

"Something's wrong here and I'm gonna figure it out." I bit her neck and groaned when she stilled. Yeah, I liked that. I wound my hands around her and jerked my hips into her ass. "I'm addicted to you. I think about you all day, and I wonder what you're doing, why you don't call me, text me, ask me how I am."

"More, Jamie, more."

"You are mine, and I am yours. That's how this works."

"I'm yours, I'm yours," she chanted, and with one final thrust, I spilled inside her.

We fell to the side.

I hugged her closer.

## CHAPTER 10

*Rey*

Something rough touched my cheek. I turned my head away and patted for Jamie next to me. The pillow was cold. I listened for the shower. The house was quiet. I sprawled all over his side and inhaled his beast scent from the pillow. "Mmm," I mumbled. My pillow smelled almost the same as his. At the grocery store, I'd get my peach shampoo and double up on the conditioner. I was lucky my hair hadn't nested in places by now since Jamie didn't use conditioner, and I needed it or my curls would knot.

Next, I stretched across the bed and reached for the thing on his nightstand. After last night, I understood Jamie better. I juggled a pair of heavy, smooth, oval-shaped balls in my hand. No, not balls, eggs. They were heavy eggs with a string joining them together. One egg was larger than the other. Now that I knew about the butt plug, I had a good idea of what Jamie wanted. He played sexy games with me, thinking about me walking around the house with things shoved up my hole or both holes, so that when he came home, I'd be crazy with want, horny as hell. Jamie enjoyed sex. I enjoyed sex with him. It tied us together.

I clicked the eggs and resolved to fit them inside me awhile before he got home. Not that I needed to be reminded of his presence when he wasn't home. I thought about him too. The way he tucked me in at night, caging my body with his before he dozed off to sleep, was my favorite time with him. Last night, after Jamie had slept, I let the silence fill the distance between us. I listened to him breathing, and when it got shallow and steady, I touched him everywhere. My fingertips explored all the muscle I couldn't see, and I imagined Jamie's back or even his chest had a wolf tattooed on it.

I imagined the wolf's lips were pulled back in a snarl. Jamie was protective, a provider, and if he'd named himself "Wolf," he must be a loyal, glorious beast. All hard muscle and big cock that stood proud and curved up to end in a wide tip. The beasts loved marking their bodies. He must have tattoos, colors on his chest and arms, meaningful memories from the past I wanted to know everything about. And I knew he had sharp claws, though they didn't hurt me.

He cared about not hurting me. In his arms, I felt safe. I'd answer for my secrets soon and come away as an ignorant wife-pair who didn't want to, or didn't care to, try to make our pairing work while doing her best to manipulate him with her pussy. Way to go, me.

I placed the eggs back on the stand and tried to go back to sleep but couldn't. He'd said we'd spend more time together. Did I want to spend more time with him already? I did. Did I still want to run away? I should want it. I carried a burden on my soul. I'd lied and manipulated a man who was good to me. Shame squeezed my heart. I needed to tell him today. Maybe he'd find a place for me. I hoped too much.

A rough thing returned, scraping my cheek. "Rey?" Jamie whispered.

"Aaah!" I nearly launched out of bed. At the last second, I gripped the end of the headboard. "I didn't hear you," I said, breathless. "What time is it?" I'd taken my watch off too. A dead giveaway.

The scent of his fresh spring-mountain soap hit my nose when he bent to nibble my ear. Such a beasty man. He liked to bite and mount me like a bitch in heat. I almost purred, thinking about last night.

"It's five in the morning," he said.

"Shoot me."

He chuckled. "Babe, there's a gray hound swimming laps in our pool."

I snapped opened my eyes and moved stray hairs away from my face. A pool! "It's a stray," I blurted. Dark and I had come to Jamie from a trailer with a room and a half where we never knew if needles and beer bottles from the night before would litter the floors and counters the morning after, where we had to lock ourselves in my bedroom, hoping like hell nobody tried to get inside when they got drunk and horny. Dark wasn't just my eyes, he was also my ears, my friend, and my muscle. Now, he swam in the pool. Our pool. I imagined his goofy face.

"It looks like the same hound I said not to bring with you. Did you go back for it yesterday? Is that why I got a present when I came home?"

"No." I shook my head.

"How did it get here?"

"He followed the bikes. I think. A woman found him and dropped him off."

"What did she say to you?"

"Nothing. It was weird. She came and went so fast, I didn't even get to thank her properly."

"If she calls again, I want to know. Or even better, if she shows up here, call me immediately."

I frowned. "Why?"

"Because I said so."

I swallowed. "Well, who is she?"

"Nobody."

"Funny you say that. That's what Dad said to his wife when he came to fuck my mom."

"Rey?"

"Yup, bastard daughter of a whore. I know shit."

"You don't know shit. Are you jealous?"

"Yeah, I'm jealous."

He flipped me to my back, and his lips pressed mine, his tongue pushing inside. It was so sudden and forceful that the only thing left to do was to open and take him. I gripped his shoulders, dug my fingers into them, and ran my tongue over his canines. My belly tingled, and I lifted my hips. Jamie moved back. "I smell needy pussy."

"Oh."

"Mm-hm. Listen, I got a thing early this morning. Get your ass dressed, and we'll go to the marketplace together. I don't wanna eat pizza anymore, and I'm sure you've had all the cake you can eat." He pecked my forehead. "I keep my promises. The woman who got your hound is somebody I'm looking for. That's all."

I smiled. "Let me keep my hound, please. I'll introduce him to our cat."

The bed dipped. Jamie sat down and ran a hand through my hair. A minute passed. "I don't know, baby, I'm not into hounds. They bark and slobber over the furniture, and I haven't seen my cat. He's probably hiding. Have you been feeding him?"

"Cake, we're having cake. He sits by the fridge and meows, begging to get his whiskers white. We're sort of bonding over the cake. Great cake."

"We'll see." A pause. "There's no girly shit in our bathroom."

"What?"

"Only a toothbrush."

He sniffed my hair. "A guy shampoo. Your pillow smells like a guy lay in it."

"And you want it to smell like a girl."

"I got enough of myself around here and—"

"Your bedroom prowess fills the room."

"Say what?" His mouth brushed the side of my neck.

"Nothing."

"You're funny in the morning." He bit.

"I have moments."

When he released my neck, he said, "I left you a note, directions on what to do with the toy on the nightstand, so that you know what it is and how it works. Read the note and do what it says, so I can mount you again tonight."

"Okay," I said. "I want to come. Many, many times."

"On my fingers. I'm gonna make you squirt." His footsteps padded to the door, where they stopped. He sighed. "I know all this is new for you, and I ain't no hearts and flowers—"

"I don't need hearts and flowers," I said. I needed someone to help me get back up on my feet. I needed a safe place. "What do you do at work?"

"Run the city."

"Thank you, Jamie. Very helpful. Do you work all days of the week?"

"I used to. Back on Tineya, no such thing as a day off. But on Earth, I try to make time for days off."

"I heard there's a fine sand beach and a huge spring-water thing like a lake right inside this city. A beast-made beach on a lake to remind you of your home. I'd like to go there, maybe learn how to swim."

Jamie stayed quiet, and for a moment I thought he'd left. Sometimes people disappeared without a word, and I ended up talking to myself. Case in point, the woman who'd brought Dark yesterday. I hadn't heard her leave.

"We live on the beach, Rey."

The door slammed closed.

---

*Jamie*

Our white three-story home sat next to Vice's home right on the water, and while our bedroom's windows overlooked the street, our balcony wrapped around the entire house with a nice big upper deck right above the patio. On the deck, I'd spent countless mornings thinking about my mate before I even knew her. Honestly, I imagined she'd be feisty and defiant. I imagined I'd discipline her day and night. For our games, of course, and not because I was an abusive dick.

Rey was a tall, curvy brunette perfection with tits that didn't even fit my large hands. A sweet girl. Yet the little shit hadn't even bothered to look outside her damn window. Just as well. I'd fuck her into wanting to stay. I'd give her so much cock, she wouldn't be able to run even if she wanted to. I shuddered at the thought of her running. I couldn't force her to stay. Mating didn't work by force.

"Your bad mood is infectious," Vice said from the rail's edge of the lighthouse where we set up our stakeout. "The sky might catch a disease and pour crap on us. Cheer up." He paced back and forth, flexing his claws. Dewlyn was driving him nuts. This morning, we watched my house from the back because Dewlyn got spooked yesterday when she'd dropped off the hound. We figured she'd come again. A girl on a mission to fuck with us. She'd intercepted a mating handover once before, and she'd probably tried to intercept mine. She'd get herself killed standing between a mated beast and his mate. We had to contain her, and Vice needed to make her his.

The last thing I wanted was for Dewlyn and Rey to get together. If Rey took off, I'd hunt her, but in the end, if she didn't want to be mated, there was nothing I could do about it. Nothing. I depended on her. I couldn't force her.

"Here's your sun-Rey. Man, this girl makes me smile," Vice said.

"Mind your own mate." I hopped on the edge and watched, the wind blowing the smell of fresh water in my face. Our eyes, made for hunting, allowed us to see a great distance. Rey stood on the porch between her small lounge chair and my bigger one. The same one I'd need to disinfect. She held the hound's leash—there went my rope—and a short white stick in her hand.

"A skinny-dip," Vice said. "Maybe I'll get an eyeful. Rawr."

"If she takes off her clothes, you're not watching. She

can't swim either, so she'll need to wait and use the pool until I teach her how to swim." Damn straight. Finally, she got out of the house and smiled a genuine smile. The same one I'd seen her wear at her compound. In turn, I showed my teeth too.

Rey jerked her hand.

The white stick unfolded into a longer stick. A cane? I tilted my head.

She placed the far end of the stick down on the ground and began tapping around. The hound plastered himself to her left leg. He stepped first, and she followed.

Vice and I both froze in place. The entire city faded before my eyes.

*Tap, tap, tap.*

I could almost hear the soft end of her cane tap the tiled edge of our pool. The myriad flashbacks assaulted me. Rey wore sunglasses most of the time. Rey avoided me. Rey didn't drive her girly bike in the city. Rey didn't look me in the eyes. Sometimes she followed my mouth and sometimes her gaze would drift not quite where it should be. At the party, she looked distracted and uncomfortable. Quiet. I attributed it to her being shy.

I blinked in disbelief.

"Bro," Vice said in a low voice.

"No." I shook my head. "Don't say it. I left her alone for days, and she didn't even know where she was."

"You're an ape. How could you not know? Oh, hold up." He raised his hand. "I know how. You took her like an ape. Ape thought banging her and swinging his cock around was all it would take. You thought that's all you had to do. I told you about the natives. These women aren't bitches. You can't just fuck them into submission, you gotta...talk. A looooot of talking about issues until your head hurts, but—"

"Shut up, Vice, I'm having a mental breakdown." I scrubbed my eyes. "She asked me to leave her alone so she could figure out how to get out before I found out. But with no... The notes. Oh shit."

"You wrote her love notes?" Vice threw his head back and laughed. She couldn't read the notes. I'd almost spanked her for not reading them, not doing the things I wanted her to do. "Yeah, have a breakdown. Ape."

I snarled in frustration.

"It's the pairing," he said. "That's why most of the mates are running. We buy them like fucking candy at the store. We put prices on our mates. Have a think. Rey? We paid real nice for her. Real sweet, that one, and paired with an ape." Vice shook his head. "It's a bad practice all around. Dewlyn will tell ya. Showed me, all right, left my ass even after I'd courted her and talked about issues."

"Courting didn't help you any, and you broke our code." Vice had explained the mating to Dewlyn.

"If you don't break yours, you're gonna regret it. You know anything about Rey?"

"Yup. She's mine." I thumped my chest.

"Apeshit."

"I'm going over there." I hopped on my bike and revved the engine.

Vice slapped a hand over my shoulder.

I bared my teeth. "Don't fuck around, my brother."

"Dewlyn will come. If you go there, she'll bail again and do something stupid, get herself killed."

He'd never forgive me. I revved the engine, pissed at

myself for not seeing what was in front of me, and hella pissed at Rey for not telling me.

I moved the bike to hover over the lighthouse.

Rey removed her shoes, and her bare feet toed the edge of the pool. The hound barked several times. I didn't think he liked her standing near the edge. I sure as fuck didn't.

The back door slid open.

Dewlyn stepped outside.

Rey startled and fell into the pool.

My heart ceased beating.

I propelled the bike over the water. It wouldn't go fast enough. When I got shoreside, I dropped onto the sand, not bothering to land my bike. My feet had never moved faster, and in a single three-hundred-foot leap, I dived after her.

At the bottom of the pool, Dewlyn tried to get Rey, but Rey was panicking and dragging them both down. Dewlyn's mane of red hair and Rey's brown one spread all around them. I couldn't see shit. So, I yanked them both by their hair. It was all I could see, the first thing I could grip. I swam up and up, and when I reached the top, I had the two by their waists on either side of me. I shook the water from my face.

Vice stood on the edge and extended his hands. He had a mean look on his face. I handed him his. "If you don't spank her blue, I will."

Dewlyn caught her breath, then kicked and screamed as Vice carried her next door.

The hound kept barking, running in circles around the pool. Rey didn't say anything, but I heard her rapid heartbeats. I bent her over the edge, where she coughed out the water from her lungs. Leaning my cheek on her back, I closed my eyes and breathed in deep. My lungs filled, and I released a slow, measured breath when I really wanted to snarl. Anger coursed through me like a living thing. It was better for us that she couldn't see the silver glow of my eyes. I wanted to war.

Water from my hair dripped on my shoulders. I gripped my towel and tightened it around me. Dark sat next to my chair and whimpered every now and then as Jamie paced around the bar area in our kitchen. If anger could be felt, I'd drown in it right now. Playing around the deep pool wasn't smart. I didn't think it was that deep. I imagined it to be a shallow pond I could dip into. It wasn't. And it wasn't because Jamie was a big beast who needed a lot of room. I kept forgetting who he was.

The refrigerator door opened. "Wanna drink?"

I barely recognized his voice. Too deep and a bit scary. "No, thank you."

"My little brother liked to drink," Jamie said. "His favorite pastime on this planet. I didn't understand it, and I hated it, but now I get it."

I heard gulping sounds, and the bottle slammed on the bar. I blinked a few times but didn't startle. "Mom partied, so I know what you mean."

Jamie gulped down another drink. "Been watching our house. The girl who brought your dog back is Vice's...pair. She left him, and I want to know what she told you."

"I don't know her at all."

"Hm." Jamie ran a claw down my shoulder. "How did

she get inside the house, Rey? I lock the house when I leave. Every single day."

I hung my head. "I test-drove the bike and forgot to engage the security when I went back inside."

Gently, he turned my chair and stepped between my bare thighs. "You what?"

"Forgot to lock..."

"No, the bike. Tell me about the bike."

"The house programmed the directions to places in the city into the phone. The house said I could hook the phone to the bike and that it'd take me where I needed to go. Like on autopilot. The marketplace. The fridge is empty, and you want MachoBeast razors. The blue ones." When he didn't say anything, I continued, "I didn't go. Obviously. I moved it up and down in the driveway. Pretended, you know." I needed to come clean.

"I'm gonna sell the bike."

I nodded.

Taking a strand of my hair, he said, "I'm braiding it." He kissed my forehead, and tears spilled from the edges of my eyes. "I watched you with the cane and the guide hound. I'm thinking the best thing for me to do is to leave and go for a ride. But I can't ride, because you might bail like Dewlyn bailed. You wanna go back to places you know. I understand. Sure is better for you. Safer where you know everything. You gonna leave me, Rey?"

"Are you gonna return me?"

Jamie dropped my hair and stepped back. "You're not a fucking piece of candy. You are mine!"

I stood too. "I'm not deaf!"

Silence resumed.

I sat back down. "My hearing is somewhat as good as

yours. I also have a great palate. I can tell different coffee brands of medium-blend coffee just by tasting it. I really *can* cook anything and make gourmet butter cookies from just sugar, butter, and flour. Dad used to say it's art. Also, I have a sixth sense for bullshit, so I know you're trying to contain your anger. You're mad."

"Fuck yes, I'm mad. Thinking of the kind of shit that could've happened... Why didn't you tell me? This isn't something to hide."

"At first, I wanted to run. But then we...we bonded as a couple. I didn't want to ruin it. I planned to tell you, but I wanted to try on my own. I can't depend on you to do everything for me. You're not my babysitter, you're my better half. I should be your better half, not your pain in the ass. I hate being a burden. I wanted to be—"

"Worth it?"

"Productive. But yes, you paid a fortune for me. I also want to bring something into our pairing. I didn't know how. Don't return me." There, I'd said it.

"I want to know why that is. What's wrong with going back? Leslie seemed nice, and your uncle is a pussy. Most girls we get wanna go back home. Your sister went back."

"She's dead, and he'll shoot me too."

"Say that again."

"He'll make me disappear. I'm useless to him. I won't entertain any of his games. I can't fuck—"

"Shhhh, don't say it," Jamie interrupted. "That's what he told you, didn't he? To shut up and put up, and that's what you've been doing. Leading me on so now I gotta decide."

"I'm sorry." I started removing my rings. I yanked them off and placed them on the counter. "It's a horrible mistake, a horrible lie, I'm a horrible person, but don't take me back. Uncle Sam lied to you about many things. I'm not worth the price you paid. He's ripped off more of your men than you'd care to know." I giggled hysterically. What I was about to tell him would doom the girls in the pairing program, but I didn't care. Someone had to speak up. "Community Seven? Damaged goods. None of us are virgins. Most of us were used goods since the day we bleed. All that glamor during the parties? It's all bullshit, Jamie. The pills? Come as a standard package for the paired brides. We all get the pills to keep cool and shut up. If you can't keep cool, they tell us to swallow the bottle. Then it's your problem to clean and not theirs. See, they have games. They herd us and make us run through the community. If you get caught, you get raped."

"Who caught you?"

"I'm a fast runner."

He cleared his throat. "How did you know where to run?"

"I could see once, until I didn't see anymore *because* I was an excellent runner."

"Tell me everything."

Sighing, I picked the ends of my hair. "One day during the hunt, I ran and hid inside the stables. My Uncle Sam found me and unzipped his pants. I kicked him in the balls. When I tried to run again, he picked up a pitchfork and swung. It caught the back of my head, and I collapsed. What he did after I passed out, I don't know, but I woke up with permanent vision damage. That's it." Jamie didn't comment, so I continued. "After, I lay in bed for months. The pills helped. Cutting helped, but I don't do that anymore. I swam out of it when Dark came around." Dark didn't make a peep. Maybe he sensed Jamie wouldn't hurt me. "This isn't what you signed up for, and I don't blame you, but I can't go back. Sam's gonna shoot me. Pop!" I mimicked a gun to my forehead. "Done. But, I don't want you to keep me because you feel sorry for me either. Not just because it's wrong, but also because we deserve better. Apart or together."

Still nothing from Jamie. I lifted my head and looked around the kitchen. "Hello? Are you there?"

"I'm here," Jamie said.

I searched the floor. He must have sat down, so I dropped to all fours and crawled to him. When I found him, I squeezed my body between his legs. "Shitty story, huh?"

Air whooshed passed me, lifting my hair.

Something crashed in the living room. I almost jumped out of my skin. My eyes blinked in rapid motion, and I felt around for the wall so I could crawl away from him. I didn't really know where I was going, just that I didn't like the sound of crashing around the house.

Jamie grabbed my hips and pulled me against him. He buried his nose into the crook of my neck. "I'm sorry about that. I'll clean it up."

"Okay."

"It'll take me a while to get used to us, and you'll need to...talk me through and tell me things. You have to know, I'd do almost anything to keep you. I never wanted you to go back. And certainly not after this."

"Thank you."

"It's not a favor. Right now I'm gonna take you upstairs, where you will remain for the rest of the day until I return. You will not try to ride the bike or go in the backyard. You will not open the door for strangers even if they're dying on the front steps. You will not do anything until I return. You can play with your pussy. That's it."

My shoulders slumped in relief. Jamie carried me upstairs. "Where are you going?"

"Hunting. Just for sport."

Wind blew inside the room when Jamie opened the window.

He howled.

# CHAPTER 11

*Jamie*

It was seven o'clock the next morning when I returned home, happy to find Rey sleeping in our bed. She liked sleeping, so I didn't bother her. I showered the blood off my hands and took some time picking off the flesh stuck behind my claws. I scrubbed my jaw. I needed a shave.

I took her purple razor and ran it over my face. I smiled at the beast in the mirror. My eyes still glowed icy cold, my teeth still in full descent, and my biceps were double their usual size.

Flesh stuck between my teeth. I threw the razor in the trash.

Floss in hand, I snuck white strand between my teeth and cleaned up..

A quiet knock on the door. "Jamie?"

"Come in, baby." I opened the door. "I'm just brushing my teeth. Your uncle stinks, but he sure was tasty."

"You ate him?"

Rey paled, so I clarified, "Not all of him. Only the good parts in the middle. My men had the rest." I threw the floss and the toothbrush in the garbage.

Despite looking sick in the face, she managed a smile. She'd get through it. I couldn't treat her like broken glass. She was a woman and my mate, and she wasn't broken. Also, I had to tell her how shit worked. "You aren't my pair, Rey. You're my mate. You are the center of my universe. That's what a mate is to a beast male. Your people damaged the center of my universe." I rinsed and spat. "I had to make a show so everyone knows what'll happen if the girls are treated the way you've been treated. We can't take all the girls from their homes. It doesn't work that way, and we need our mates. We shut down Community Seven." Rey gaped at me. I shrugged. They hated us, and they'd hurt the girls because they couldn't hurt us. "It's over, and I got shit to do on that front, but me and you? We're starting over. Let's do it. Wanna get dressed and go to the marketplace?"

"Wha... Yeah, uh-huh."

"Good, 'cause I ain't going there by myself. Markets give me the creeps."

"You ate my uncle, but the market gives you the creeps?"

"Mm-hm. Get dressed." I slapped her ass as I walked by. "I'm in the walk-in." She followed my voice. I could do this. We'd be fine. "All right, Rey. How much can you see? Anything?"

"Contrasting colors and you. I can see you. A big dark mass under the lamp."

"So I *am* a black blob in your space, then?"

Chuckling, she searched for clothes in the laundry basket. She didn't have anything clean left.

"Wear one of my T-shirts," I said.

"It's too big."

I got a black shirt anyway, and a belt, then dressed her. The shirt's hem reached to her knees, and Rey was a tall girl with long legs. Man, she was sexy, and my cock hardened. I was an animal. No wonder some girls took off running at a sight of their mates.

She fiddled with the belt. "You *do* have belts. Where are they?"

"The shelf on top of the rack."

Rey rose on her toes and reached up. "How tall are you?" she asked.

"I'm big."

"How big?"

"Thirteen inches." I didn't want to tell my height or weight. I didn't want her to picture a beast, I wanted her to *see* me. She strained, the hem of her shirt rising. "You can't reach it. Need a step stool, which I will not provide. You're clumsy."

She gasped. "I am not."

I chuckled.

"This is a woman's belt." Rey blushed, but not from being shy. I whistled a low tune, liking her jealousy. I still hadn't forgiven her for telling me to go bang other women on my mating night. "Well, whose is it?"

"Do you really want to know?"

She flung her hair over her shoulder. "I do."

"Mom's. She visits with us. Leaves things so she doesn't have to bring them along every time."

"I'd like to meet her."

"You will."

"Are you dressed?" she asked and ran a finger down my stomach.

My cock sprang up as if called to service. Rey dropped

to her knees and gripped it. I found her eyes when she looked up, and her little tongue swirled around the tip, testing. Gentle hands stroked me, and I could barely feel her grip. "It's not gonna break. Shove it inside until it chokes you, and suck the life out it. That's all there is to it." Never in a million years would I ask her if she'd done this before. And not only because I knew she hadn't. If she had, they wouldn't have hurt her. Man, I'd eat that motherfucker again if I could. The natives call us beasts and said our females shouldn't be called bitches. Fuck them. No bitch got hurt in this city.

I snarled.

Rey paused.

"No, baby. It's fine." I gripped her hair and guided her to fill her mouth. Her hand landed on my thigh when I moved back and forth. It was like she knew I needed this after a bad night. I wanted to feel her, and I wanted to know we'd be fine. The emotional crap gave me the creeps, and this was all I knew how to do. But Rey was all soft and sweet, and she'd make up for the two of us. I took her hand and put it on my balls so she could play around. When Rey gagged, I thrust again. She gagged some more, and I liked that because I was a sadistic prick.

I guided her head. It bobbed until I came down her throat. Kneeling with her, I kissed her on the mouth.

"Mmm," she said. "It's bitter."

"Get used to it. You getting used to it?"

The smile caught the corners of her eyes. I wanted to fuck her for days. But she was hungry, and so was I. We needed to get going. "I'm gonna invade your space, and when I do"—I played my fingers over her wet slit—"you're gonna like it."

She took my face between her hands, and her smile

vanished. Her fingertips roamed over my nose and my mouth, my neck and my arms. "You've grown," she said.

"It happens."

"Did he die a slow and painful death?" she asked.

"Very slow and painful."

"Hm."

I quit messing around. She had something on her mind. Maybe telling her we ate people wasn't such a great idea.

"Do you have tattoos?" she asked.

My eyebrows drew down. "Yeah, I got many."

When her palms cupped my face and tears filled her eyes, a feeling of foreboding came over me. I'd come at her like a semitruck when I should've come like a moped. Nice, small, and slow. I felt a hole in my chest. I couldn't do this. I couldn't keep my mate. She was too sweet, and I was too... me. We had nothing in common. How was I gonna do this?

"I love you, Jamie," she told me.

Motherfucker. I lunged at her and buried myself to the hilt.

I made love to her. Love. *That's right.* In confirmation, I grunted.

## CHAPTER 12

*Rey*

Jamie was at least a head taller than my five foot nine, so that put him at about six foot four. When he walked, he marched with long strides. Of course, with my hand in his, I jogged. Doors slid open, and cold air swept my skin. Goose bumps rose over my bare shoulders. The market was cold. Abruptly, Jamie stopped, and I ran into his bicep.

Soft lips pressed my forehead. "Got a list or somethin'?"

I nodded. "The house made a list for me." I reached into my backpack and passed him the home phone. "Command: Grocery list," I spoke into the odd appliance I called a home phone.

For a while, Jamie was quiet, and then he said, "This isn't a grocery list. It's a fucking book."

"What's it about?" I asked, messing with him. It'd been a month since we'd come clean to each other. The weight of our secrets had suffocated us for the first few days of our mating, but not anymore. It could've been great from the start, if only we hadn't hidden from each other. Mating was such a nice bond, much better than pairing. It made me feel owned and loved and, most importantly, safe. Jamie loved me. I didn't need words to tell me that when I had his actions. Jamie took care of me.

"The book is about this Alpha Beast, who went to the store and ended up in one of his own jails." He huffed and puffed at the list, then strode away. I followed, my hand in his. "The veggies are on the right," he said. He placed my hands on something soft. Tomatoes. "Pick those. I got... eggplant. I didn't know eggs grew out of the ground around here."

"They don't."

"So it must look like an egg, then."

I pictured him searching for the vegetable. "Not really. Eggplant is big, smooth, and purple. You can't miss it."

"So it looks like a tortured dick. Anyway, what's it for?" he asked.

"I was gonna make you moussaka."

"Say that again."

"It's Greek."

"I don't eat dick plants. Forget it. Make me a steak. I'll get potatoes."

"No, wait. Moussaka is delicious, and I have a great recipe from Grans. It has ground beef in it."

"No eggplant."

"I want you to try it. It comes in layers, and eggplant is one of them."

"No problem. Layer the thing with potatoes. No eggplant. Wait a minute. Light salad dressing? I don't think so."

"Baked chips," I said, firmly. "And pads with wings." I waited for his horrified response. His boots stomped, and a minute later, a bag—potatoes, likely—hit the bottom of the cart. "Done. Let's get pads."

We moved around.

"You don't mind getting pads?" I asked.

"Nope."

Awww.

"You can't be bleeding all over the furniture. I got you covered, baby." We stopped. "Hold on, they got a whole aisle for this shit, and fifty of them got wings. Your peach gonna fly." Jamie amused himself.

"Hi, there," a woman said. "Can I help you?"

"Yes," I said. "Could you get me Jazzies number three with wings?"

"Over here. Which package?"

"Thirty-six pack."

"I'm sorry, we're all out. Here are the smaller ones, or we have a large pack in another brand." I was sure she pointed them out. Jamie took my hands and put packaged pads in them. "What's the difference between these two?" I asked.

Silence resumed.

Jamie tapped his foot. "Today?"

"Um, um..."

If you didn't know Jamie like I did, you'd be scared of him. The woman was probably terrified. Dressed in leathers, with his wolfy eyes and big teeth, Jamie was a menace. Not to mention he was the Alpha Beast of Beast City. At least he hadn't "minded" her.

I opened my mouth to say either of the pads would do

when Jamie said, "Mind. She asked what's the difference, and you're looking at me like I got answers. I don't have a pussy. You do, and I bet it bleeds. Pads?"

"Um..."

"My peach hears fine, but if you um and hum, she can't understand. I can't understand. Fuck it. I got the pads. One of each brand." Pads flew out of my hands. Boots shuffled away. "The fuck is wrong with..." He sniffed loudly. "Baby, there's perfume on this thing."

"Some women like—"

"No scented pads for you. Wings, no scent. A large pack."

*Thunk. Thunk. Thunk.*

The packs landed in the cart. "What else? Let's see." He read, "A medium-size pack. Got it. No panty liners. No underwear for you on off days. What's next? Hound food. We'll buy him pussy food. He chewed my boot, then hid under the bed like a pussy. Did you know that?"

"I'll talk to him about the shoes."

"How?"

"I have a way with animals."

Jamie cupped my cheek, stroked it with his thumb, and I leaned into his palm. "Yeah, you do," he said.

An announcement broke the spell, and we moved again.

"Whatcha staring at?" Jamie shouted. "Fuck off to the next aisle. Hurry up, baby, people are looking at you, and I'm gonna have you roast somebody."

"I'm pretty sure they're looking at you."

"Why?"

"This city is yours. You're grunting and stomping in the girly aisle. It makes people nervous."

"You know what? I'm gonna put you in the cart," he declared.

"The shopping cart?"

"Mm-hm."

"It's better if we don't draw any more attention."

"We're not. I'm gonna put you in the cart and push you to the deli, where we're gonna grab sandwiches and eat them at home."

"And what should we eat tomorrow?"

"I'll get someone to do this for us and deliver it to the door. Wouldn't you like that better?"

I laughed when he plopped me down to sit inside the cart. He propelled us forward, cutting corners left and right with my hair flying all over my face. I gripped the sides of the cart and laughed.

Mid-run, Jamie said, "Baby, we gonna spin. Remember how we spin? Hang on."

"No, we don't have to do that."

"Hang on."

"Aaaaahhh!"

Jamie laughed and, a spin later, stopped at the deli. "Can I help you?" the woman asked.

Jamie read the entire menu for me.

Life dealt me a wild card, I thought. Jamie was my wild card.

***

Hello, Milana here. I want to take ten seconds and

thank you for reading Blind Beast Mate. And extend my thanks to my beta reader AJ who's read my books since 2014 (before I published) and my super awesome editor Linda and her team who clean up my words. I own all the typos found.

If you enjoyed Jamie and Rey's story, please leave a word or two as a review on your favorite book site. On the next page, sneak a peak at Wild Beast Mate. Dewlyn is fire, and Vice is oh so yummy.

# WILD BEAST MATE

## Dewlyn

You'd think by this day and age, the beasts who took over the earth after the Great Nuclear War would bring us humans out-of-the-world advanced technology. Like they could come up with some sort of a universal key set for burglars, a shape-changing key that molded to every lock you jabbed it into so that I wouldn't have to swipe hairpins from random women as I swooped from the sky. Just sayin'.

At midnight, inside the dark office space of a recently built high-rise in the city once called Louisville, I dreamed of a universal key set as I picked a tiny little lock with hairpins I'd gotten from Rey, my sister-in-law, before I ran away from Vice, my beast mate. Before I ran away from him the *second* time. The first time, after Vice had proclaimed me his mate and not just a pair he'd bought because of my red hair, petite body, and pixie face, I'd knocked him out in his sleep and run. I'd just wanted him to leave me alone. But he hadn't.

The second time, he caught me when I tried to rescue Rey from drowning. Then he got smart and put me in a cage at night while he slept. But one morning, while Vice showered, my sister-in-law—bless her good heart—gave me her hairpins. I picked the cage's lock, freeing myself, then took to the skies with her unused horrific pink bike. For a few days, I huddled inside the shelter I'd set up for me and other runaway pairs. Until we ran out of food, and, again, I needed to get out there and get some.

Luckily, my friend Patty, our house sister, got news from her boyfriend just as I set out to raid fridges and pantries in the Beast City. He'd heard of New City, a city on the rise, and located a storage place where the construction workers got their food supplies. That much food? So worth checking out, and so I traveled to New City.

At first, I scouted New City for a temporary home, and once I found one, I scouted the construction company's building. Now I readied to rob the construction manager's office of the key to the storage place. However temporary my stay might be, I welcomed the relocation into New City. Vice flew over the Beast City, relentless in his pursuit to bring me in and lock me up inside his house. So my mission out here in the middle of Nowhere, Kentucky, afforded me an opportunity to get away from his big hands.

The beige paint on the office walls, the leather furniture and polished metal desk, along with a new carpet decorating the office all stank with that telltale new smell. I pulled the hem of my T-shirt over my nose.

Beyond the wide window behind me, most of New City rested in quiet slumber. On the ground floor, four hundred and twenty feet below my feet, the security guards snored at their posts. Maybe not both of them, but I knew at least one snored away while the other tried to keep his eyes open, alert to the monotony of the empty building on a monitor before him.

Since escaping Vice, I'd observed many guards, detailed many buildings back in the Beast City. When I first left Vice, and without a roof over my head, I'd survived by scavenging the Dumpsters and sleeping inside empty homes. Then I found an abandoned basement right under a bakery and spent a few weeks hiding in there, coming up only long enough to hoard some food. One day, I met Patty, another runaway, who knew her shit around the kitchen. Together we founded the very first and only Shelter from the Beasts. The shelter hid paired woman who'd refused pairings, and we've since grown to eighteen women. And all those mouths needed to eat.

My stomach growled.

It might as well be a beast in its own right, I was so hungry. I jabbed the pin, trying to force the lock open. The pin snapped. I flicked the broken piece. I popped my knuckles and adjusted my backpack, then crouched, eye level with the desk drawer where I hoped I'd find the storage key. If the key wasn't in the drawer, the next option was the safe inside the wall. If it was in there, I'd need to blow the safe door. When it exploded, the guards would figure out someone up here was robbin' their asses, so I'd need to drug them before blowing shit up. I really hoped the manager hadn't felt the need to hide the key.

I jabbed a pair of new hairpins inside the small lock, then fiddled with the metal until a click sounded in the silent room. Sweat accumulated on my forehead, and I dabbed it on my sleeve, then peeked inside the drawer. Winner winner chicken dinna! Literally. I haven't had a chicken in like...months, ever since I'd escaped Vice for the first time.

The key was a rectangular plastic card half the size of my palm. It was smooth and transparent, but much thicker than the keys beasts used in the city. It looked outdated. I pocketed it, then peeked back inside the drawer. Oh, a protein bar! I unwrapped it. Sitting down cross-legged, I bit into the delicious morsel. Mmmm, orange flakes and nuts coated in chocolate.

The dust played above the carpet as my flashlight searched the room.

*Shit.* I swallowed and tilted my head, listening.

From the hallway, the security guard shouted, "Got a light alert for twenty-three zero five."

What light? I looked around the room. Sure enough, a tiny night lamp shone dimly in the corner of the room. The motion sensors in the office had worked, and the lamp had lit up while I busied myself with the picks.

The door handle jerked.

I peeked over the desk and stuck my hand into my pocket.

The security guard, in a black uniform, fiddled with the lock. I took a few seconds to size him up, and unfortunately, the beast was fit, which meant he wouldn't tire as quickly as an unfit beast. Time to go. I crawled across the office space to the adjacent suite's polished, dark wooden door.

Above my head, the flashlight hit the door. "Got a guy in here!"

Before the building locked down, I opened the door, then turned. When the beast stepped inside, I got a short blowgun from my pocket and pressed it over my lips.

He advanced.

I blew.

Hit! Right in the neck.

The beast wouldn't collapse, but the poisoned dart

would slow him down. Adjusting my pack, I ran to the other office's exit door, skipping the visitors' chairs in my way.

The lights lit up the hallway.

The alarms blared through the building.

Feet pounded the carpeted floors. "Stop!"

Not a chance! I wasn't getting caught again.

Small round lights above the metal doors signaled that the elevator was on the first floor, so I ran to the fire exit at the end of the hallway, the guard on my heels. Or was it both guards by now? I didn't look back, only forward.

"Climbing up!" the guard shouted.

The alarms triggered the lockdown right after I opened the exit door.

Leaping three stairs at the time, heart pounding, I fisted my hands and worked my shoulders and legs twenty floors to the roof The beasts were big, bulky guys, so I sprinted. Quick on my feet, I got to the top and kicked the exit door. Locked. *Shit.*

I heaved breaths along with the guard, who panted as he climbed the stairs, the poison rushing through his bloodstream. From my other pocket, I got a tiny detonator and pasted it like a piece of gum on the door right above the lock. I stepped back, covered my ears. *Three, two, one. Boom!* Blew the lock. I'd have used that on the safe's door.

I pushed past the door and stepped onto the roof. Heaving breaths, mouth gaping, I propped my hands on my knees and checked the area. Full-moon light graced the star-filled winter night skies. In the distance, a giant beast ship hovered over the city. The battle cruiser looked like it would touch the moon. Beneath the ship and inside the city on top of the hills, a few stray cars passed through the night. That small neighborhood was my destination.

"Nowhere to go, man," the wounded guard said from the bottom of the last staircase.

I leapt onto the edge of the building and yanked off my hat. My long red braid bounced off the middle of my back. "What's up, beasty mofo? I ain't no guy."

Vice

Thousands of feet above the city, in the surveillance room of my battle cruiser, I rested my elbows on my knees and leaned in as if I couldn't clearly see the scene unfolding before me on the giant screen. My mate, Dewlyn, had escaped our home again. I'd chased after her, then ordered my males to sweep the city every single hour. They'd swept for weeks and come up with nothing. It was as if she'd crawled into a hole and hadn't come up for air.

When the wait for her to surface got too long, I flew back to my battle cruiser, dropped the ship closer to Earth, and used the air traffic search sensors to sweep for small bikes such as the one Dewlyn had stolen from my brother's mate. Thousands of small vehicles registered. I waited for one pink bike.

Patience paid off, and I got lucky. Yesterday, a small pink bike had popped up in New City. Dewlyn rode that thing like she rode everything else: hard and fast. And so here I was with my ship's surveillance crew. My brother followed, his mate, Rey, in tow.

Next to me, the chair protested as my brother Jamie, the Alpha Beast, leaned closer to the screen too. His eyebrows drew down. "You took her hydro-skater, didn't you?"

"Mm-hm," I mumbled.

"And she doesn't seem to have Rey's bike with her."

"Should've sold that damn thing when you had the chance."

Jamie pierced me with one of his glares. If I hadn't grown up with this asshole, I would've pissed myself. But I had grown up with him, and also our father, so I kept staring at the screen, ignoring the glare.

"If she doesn't have transport," he said, "what the fuck is she doing on the edge of the building?"

I shrugged. "The fuck if I know."

"If this was Rey, I'd have gone mad already."

"You are mad. There's no need to go anywhere." I watched the screen. The guard—finally!—caught up with her. He heaved breaths, one hand holding the side of his neck. When he saw her standing on the edge, his eyebrows shot up, and he showed her his empty hands. This beast was about five feet ten inches, with a shaved head and large hoop earrings. Medrix. I'd make him run laps for a week. Maybe then he'd build up some stamina. I popped my knuckles, wanting to break his face.

"All right, bitch, listen up," he said. "Don't be jumping on my watch. I can't have it." He motioned with his hand to the exit. "You can walk. Just don't jump. It's not worth it."

Dewlyn pointed to the two-inch-wide black leather collar around her neck. My collar. The white inscription one could read from five hundred fucking miles away but Medrix had missed, read: *Property of Vice, Tineyas Second.*

Wide-eyed, Medrix swallowed. "A pair," he said. "You're Vice's pair. Do not fucking jump on my watch!"

"I won't if you give him a message."

Both Jamie and I approached the screen. I swiped a hand over it. "Zoom in," I commanded.

Man, she was something. All of four feet eleven, with her long red braid swaying in the wind, smiling big brown eyes, dirty jeans, and a dirty white T-shirt over her pear-shaped, honed body, she was fire contained in a tiny, sexy box. I needed to open up that box, have it spill its secrets without burning us both. She didn't make it easy on me, and I didn't know why.

A glint in her eye warned me something wicked had just crossed her mind. A cold shiver ran through my body. Dewlyn pulled on the belts strapped around her thigh.

"What's she doing?" Jamie asked.

I shrugged again.

She glanced down, to probably over six hundred feet below. A knot of fear formed in my throat.

"Tell Vice I want him to leave me alone," she said. "Tell him I hate him."

"Bullshit," I argued with the screen.

Medrix advanced.

"Don't come closer, or I'll go over," she said.

"She's messing with him," I whispered. *Right?*

Jamie snorted.

"Come back down," Medrix said. "I swear I'll let you walk out of here. You running from Vice? I won't tell him you're here. Just don't jump."

Under her feet, she kicked back the loose cement when her toes crossed the building's edge. Below, a few lights twinkled, and to the right was an empty parking platform. Dewlyn smiled.

"Is she suicidal?" Jamie asked.

Maybe, but I'd never tell a living soul. "Nah. Adrenaline junkie. She'll come back down when he quits begging."

"Disaster, Vice. She's a fucking disaster."

"Don't talk about her like that."

"What the fuck is she doing on the edge of that building? Why are you all cool about it? Wait, don't answer that. You've lost your shit, that's why." Jamie stood and began pacing the surveillance room. We'd moved from Earth back into the ship so we could observe Dewlyn instead of chase her. This view was healthier for her, seeing as she was hell-bent on running from me and running our lives.

But I would have her back. I would have her back, and I would isolate us from all life. I had to tame her. Nothing else would do.

"See ya!" She leapt off the edge.

*What?!* My chest constricted. My heart didn't beat as her body dropped. I gasped, struggling to catch a breath, not knowing if I should continue watching, or turn away so I wouldn't see her splatter on the asphalt. My body, frozen by the scene before me, my eyes frozen in time, my brain blank, made the decision for me. I couldn't fucking move. CLICK IT!

## *ABOUT THE AUTHOR*

Milana Jacks grew up with tales of water fairies that seduced men, vampires that seduced women, and Babaroga who'd come to take her away if she didn't eat her bean soup. She writes dystopian sci-fi romance with dominant monsters from her home on Earth she shares with Mate and their three little beasts.

• Sometimes she releases stories for the readers on her mailing list as they await for books in the series. If you want in, join other readers here : http://www.milanajacks.com/newsletter/ •

MILANA JACKS
DOMINANT MONSTERS

*Meet me at*
www.milanajacks.com

## *MILANA'S BACKLIST*

Dirty Wolf, Jake, and Alpha Thief are exclusive to my newsletter subscribers.

http://www.milanajacks.com/newsletter/

**Read the complete Beast Mates Series:**

#0 Virgin - FREEBIE, #1 Blind, #2 Wild,

#2.5 Goddess, FREE via my Mailing List,

#3 Sent, #3.5 Their, #4 Caught, #4.5 His, #5 Free.

**Read the Alpha Horde Series:**

Alpha Breeds #1, Alpha Bonds #2

**Read the complete Dragon Brotherhood:**

Rise for Her #1, Burn for Her #2, Storm for Her #3, Fight for Her, #4

Short stories in IADB World: Jake 1.5, Eddy #2.5

**Dirty Monsters (can be read out of order)**

Real Good Wolf #1, Lonely Vampire Prince #2

**Jade Dober dystopian urban fantasy series:**

#1 Mediator Seeks, #2 Mediator Tricks

Printed in Dunstable, United Kingdom

73424870R00063